Maddie shivered, realising they were trapped.

"He's after me. He knows I went into the woods. He knows I saw."

Shane nodded and pulled her into his arms again. "The sheriff will find him."

Her limbs trembled. She couldn't remember ever feeling this weak and exhausted or this relieved to see anyone. She leaned into him, feeling his warmth and his strength.

Shane was here to rescue her. That's what a true lawman did.

All he'd ever wanted was to protect her. But she'd been so certain she could take care of herself – that she had no other choice. Now her eyes burned with tears and it took all of her strength not to cry.

But before she could take another breath, she heard the roar of an engine and a bullet whizzed through the air next to them…

Available in July 2010
from Mills & Boon® Intrigue

Tall Dark Defender
by Beth Cornelison
&
Stealing Thunder
by Patricia Rosemoor

Manhunt in the Wild West
by Jessica Andersen
&
Tycoon Protector
by Elle James

Dark Guardian
by Jan Hambright
&
Terms of Engagement
by Kylie Brant

Shotgun Bride
by BJ Daniels

SHOTGUN BRIDE

BY
BJ DANIELS

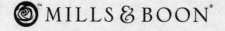

™ MILLS & BOON®

First published in Great Britain 2010
Harlequin Mills & Boon Limited,
Eton House, 18-24 Paradise Road, Richmond, Surrey TW9 1SR

© Barbara Heinlein 2009

ISBN: 978 0 263 88241 4

46-0710

Harlequin Mills & Boon policy is to use papers that are natural, renewable and recyclable products and made from wood grown in sustainable forests. The logging and manufacturing processes conform to the legal environmental regulations of the country of origin.

Printed and bound in Spain
by Litografia Rosés S.A., Barcelona

BJ Daniels wrote her first book after a career as an award-winning newspaper journalist and author of thirty-seven published short stories. That first book, *Odd Man Out*, received a 4½ star review from *Romantic Times BOOKreviews* magazine and went on to be nominated for Best Intrigue for that year. Since then she has won numerous awards, including a career achievement award for romantic suspense and many nominations and awards for best book.

Daniels lives in Montana with her husband, Parker, and two springer spaniels, Spot and Jem. When she isn't writing, she snowboards, camps, boats and plays tennis. Daniels is a member of Mystery Writers of America, Sisters in Crime, Thriller Writers, Kiss of Death and Romance Writers of America.

To contact her, write to BJ Daniels, PO Box 1173, Malta, MT 59538, USA or e-mail her at bjdaniels@mtintouch. net. Check out her website, www.bjdaniels.com.

This book is dedicated to the readers who love the fictional town of Whitehorse, Montana, and its residents as much as I do. Say hello to the Corbett family.

Chapter One

Jerilyn Larch froze, one foot on the floor.

From the sagging motel bed, Earl Ray Pitts mumbled something, let out a snort and resumed snoring loudly.

Jerilyn released the breath she'd been holding and slipped out of the bed, knowing she'd called this one a little too close.

Gingerly she picked up each piece of her clothing from the grimy carpet and tiptoed into the bathroom to get dressed.

Jerilyn Larch hadn't just fallen on hard times. She'd hit rock bottom. While the Larch name had once meant something in this part of Arizona, it wasn't worth squat anymore.

The land was gone and so was the money. Worse, as her mother would have said, Jerilyn had hooked up with the wrong sort. She needed to get out of this ratty motel—out of this town—as quickly as possible and put some miles between her and the man still in the lumpy double bed.

Dressed, she peered out of the bathroom. Only a

little of the gray dawn leaked through the cheap drapes. Earl Ray was still sleeping or at least pretending to. She could never tell for sure with him. The man had a mean streak that she knew all too well. He'd told her often enough that he'd kill her if she ever left him—or at least make her wish she was dead.

For days she'd been looking for a chance to escape.

She glanced around for his keys and caught sight of herself in the filmed-over mirror by the door, shocked by what she saw: a woman who looked much older than forty-two, a woman with nothing to lose. Jerilyn silently made a promise to herself. Her life was going to get better, starting today.

Spying the keys on the bureau, she carefully picked them up and hesitated for a moment before she scooped up Earl Ray's wallet.

Slipping out, she hustled to his Buick parked in front of the room. The car was old, the rear panels rusted, a real embarrassment. She wished that if she had to borrow a car, she could at least get one that was worth a damn. But beggars couldn't be choosers, and she had the keys to this one.

Jerilyn climbed behind the wheel and made a quick check of the wallet. Earl Ray didn't have enough money to get her far. She tossed the wallet on the seat and felt herself panic as she considered what her options were with little money, a car that probably wouldn't get her past town and nowhere to run.

Earl Ray would be furious. He was mean enough, but taking his money and his car and then leaving him high and dry in some tiny sand-blown desert town would push him over the edge. As if he needed a nudge.

As she sat there, a realization began to set in. Once she started this car and made a run for it, she'd have to look out for herself. And that frightened her almost more than Earl Ray did.

Jerilyn had always latched on to a man and let him make all the decisions for her. Earl Ray was a bastard, but maybe being on her own was worse. She glanced toward the motel room, wondering if she could slip back inside without him noticing she'd ever left.

As if in answer, the door banged open, and Earl Ray staggered out looking like this side of hell. The look on his face when he spotted her sitting behind the wheel of his car told her there would be no turning back.

Jerilyn stabbed the key into the ignition and cranked up the engine. The radio blasted on, drowning out whatever he was yelling.

Throwing the car into Reverse, she hit the gas as he lunged for the Buick. He fell face-first onto the gravel as she sped backward, nearly taking out a palm tree.

Slamming the car into Drive, she barely missed Earl Ray as she took off, tires spitting gravel as the vehicle fishtailed.

At the street, she stopped, opened the window and, after snatching out the cash, tossed his wallet in the dirt.

She might have hit bottom, but Jerilyn Larch was no thief. The three hundred and seventy-eight dollars she'd taken was money earned from putting up with him.

As for the car, well, she'd call him once this was over and let him know where to find it—no doubt abandoned beside some road where the engine had quit for good.

In her rearview mirror, she could see that Earl Ray was up on his feet and stumbling after her. Jerilyn hit the gas and didn't look back again. She knew he couldn't call the police to report the car stolen, not in his line of work as a thug between illegal crime jobs.

Maybe he wouldn't even come after her. Maybe all those threats had been nothing but bluster. Either way, she'd have to move quickly, staying one step ahead of him until she could escape the country.

She would ditch the car once she reached Montana—if the car made it that far. Otherwise, she'd hitch-hike. It wouldn't be the first time. She just hoped it would be the last.

Montana. Jerilyn hadn't realized she'd made a decision where to go until that moment. She'd promised herself years ago that she wouldn't use what she considered her ace in the hole unless she was truly desperate.

Well, she was desperate now, she thought, as she reached into her shoulder bag and removed the small, beaded purse her grandmother had given her. Most of the beads were missing, the fabric beneath gray with age.

She nearly ran off the road as she unzipped the purse and pulled out the piece of yellowed paper.

She had to hold it for a moment just to make sure the note was still there and that she hadn't made it up like she had that rosy future she dreamed about all the time.

The writing had faded from age and too much

handling, but as she held it up to the light, she saw with relief that she could still make out the words.

Guilt pierced her conscience, but she cast it aside as quickly as she had Earl Ray at the motel and the man before him. Jerilyn returned the note to her purse just as carefully as she had twenty-six years ago.

A male orderly had handed her the note the day she'd given birth. Sixteen and pregnant. Just a baby herself. Her hips were too narrow, and the doctors had to take the baby, leaving her sterile and scarred in ways that had never healed.

Her mama had made it clear from the start that she couldn't keep the baby. Jerilyn was too young, too immature, to raise a child.

"You'd just mess up the poor baby's life as you have your own," her mother had predicted. "I'm doing that baby the biggest favor of its life."

Jerilyn hated her mother for those words. She knew the real truth. Her mama didn't want the Larch name tarnished by some illegitimate baby. That's why she made Jerilyn go away to Montana before anyone knew she was pregnant.

After the birth, she'd gotten only a glimpse of the tiny pink toes peeking out of the blanket before her mama handed the infant off to some old woman down the hall.

That same night, there was another young girl in labor. Later, Jerilyn had heard her crying as if her heart was also breaking.

"Your baby is with a good family, a family with money and status, a family like ours was before you disgraced us all," her mama had said when Jerilyn begged for information about her baby. "The less you know the better. Just forget you ever had it."

As if her mama had ever let her forget. The Larch family seemed to be cursed after that. Her father made some bad investments and everything went downhill from there. Of course, her mother blamed her although no one knew about the tiny little baby girl she'd been forced to give up.

That was the first time Jerilyn had known heartbreak, but definitely not the last.

The adoption had all been done in secret. There was no paperwork and no chance of Jerilyn ever finding out what had happened to her little girl.

At least that's what her mama had thought until her dying day.

But her mama had no idea what she was capable of when she put her mind to it. Jerilyn had paid the sympathetic orderly to get her information, and he came back with a scrap of yellow paper.

On the paper was written:

Baby girl: Madeline "Maddie" Cavanaugh to Sarah and Roy Cavanaugh, Old Town Whitehorse, Montana.

Now Jerilyn was about to right the terrible wrong her mother had forced her to commit.

"I'm finally going to find my girl," she said as she steered the Buick north toward Montana. Jerilyn hoped that her mama had been right about one thing—that her baby had gone to a good family, a generous one with money and status.

Being a friendly family would help, too, but if not, Jerilyn imagined they would pay to get rid of her.

Jerilyn hated what she was about to do, but in a way she'd felt as if it was out of her hands, as if it had been destined since she was sixteen.

EARL RAY LISTENED to the knock of his old Buick's engine as it faded away in the distance. What the hell was the woman thinking? No one was that stupid, were they?

He waited, hoping the car blew a rod before it disappeared from view, or that Jerilyn had the good sense to turn around and come back.

Otherwise there was going to be serious trouble.

Earl Ray accepted partial responsibility for the situation. Last night at the bar he'd seen a man he'd thought he recognized. Worrying that it was someone after him and the little black book, he'd slipped the leather notebook into Jerilyn's shoulder bag.

When he'd realized there was nothing to worry about, he decided to leave the book in her purse until he could retrieve it without Jerilyn being any the wiser. Jerilyn was the last person he wanted knowing anything about the book—or its contents.

Unfortunately, he'd let himself drink too much and had forgotten about retrieving it. Now the stupid broad had taken off with the book, not even realizing that she had it.

At least he didn't think she did.

Either way, she had something equivalent to a bomb in her purse. That book was his ticket out of this miserable existence he'd been living. There was only one problem. If the book fell into the wrong hands, he was a dead man.

Earl Ray let out a string of expletives. If he could have gotten his hands on Jerilyn, he would have wrung her neck. The good news was that she couldn't get far in that pile of rusted junk.

As he started back toward the room, he realized he should have known she was going to take off. In the past when she became weepy drunk, she'd take out that little coin purse of hers and look at a scrap of faded paper. Lately, she'd been looking at it more and more.

The first time he'd seen her crying over the note, he'd waited until she passed out and dug the damned thing out of her purse, thinking the dumb broad was crying over some man.

It didn't take a genius to figure out what the note was about—or where Jerilyn was now headed. This had been coming for some time, and Earl Ray prided himself on knowing women.

He limped into his motel room and closed the door behind him. Luckily, he knew where he could scrape up some money and help. He picked up the phone and dialed his associates Bubba and Dude, his anger ebbing a little as he realized the three of them could beat Jerilyn to Montana.

Earl Ray smiled. He couldn't wait to see her face.

Chapter Two

"I say we settle this with a horse race."

"The hell we will," Dalton Corbett said, pushing his brother Jud out of the way in order to get to the bar in the main house on the Trails West Ranch.

Jud might have been the youngest of the Corbett brothers—three minutes behind his fraternal twin, Dalton—but in no way was he the smallest. Not at six foot three! The Hollywood stuntman was like all the Corbett brothers: tall and broad-shouldered, handsome as sin and wild as the West Texas wind.

Jud shoved Dalton back, and the two commenced pushing and jostling just as they'd done as boys.

"Hell, let's just shoot it out," Shane said. He stepped past the two to grab a glass and a bottle of bourbon from behind the bar before settling into one of the deep leather chairs. He looked out a bank of windows onto the rolling prairie of Montana. Only the purple silhouette of the Little Rockies broke the wide expanse of open range.

Shane wondered what the hell his father had been

thinking, moving here. Grayson Corbett hadn't been thinking clearly, that was the only thing that could explain it. That and the fact that his father, at the ripe old age of fifty-five, had fallen in love again.

"The only fair way to do this is to have the oldest brother go first," Lantry Corbett suggested, since he was the second to the oldest and the divorce lawyer.

Russell stood up from where he'd been sitting. "We'll draw straws." He was the oldest of the five Corbett brothers and considered the least wild of the bunch, which wasn't saying much.

Jud and Dalton quit wrestling to look at Russell. "Straws?" they asked in unison.

"Why not beans?" Shane suggested, thinking of the Texas Rangers who were caught in Mexico back in the 1800s. "A white bean, you're spared. A black bean, you're not."

"Drawing straws is the only fair way," Russell insisted, ignoring Shane's sarcasm. "We leave it up to chance."

"Or destiny," Jud added.

"*Destiny?* You've been hanging out with those Hollywood types too long," Lantry said. He grabbed a beer from behind the well-stocked bar and pulled up a chair in front of the window next to Shane.

"What do *you* say?" Lantry asked him.

Shane was disgusted with the whole mess. He poured himself a glass of bourbon and downed it before he finally spoke. "This is emotional blackmail, and I don't want any part of it."

His brothers all looked at him in surprise.

"It was our mother's dying wish," Russell said.

"Yeah, and bad karma if we ignore it," Jud said.

"Destiny? Karma?" Shane scoffed.

"It isn't just about Mom," Russell said quietly. "Can't you see what this is really about? Dad wants us here in Montana with him. He's not always going to be around."

"Well, I think he was a fool to leave Texas," Shane said.

Russell shook his head. "He did it for Kate. He loves her and would do anything for her. Look how happy Dad is. All those years of being lonely without Mom. I'm glad he found Kate."

"Kate found him," Shane corrected. "Just to keep the record straight."

This marriage and the move to Montana had been all her doing. Anyone could see that. She'd gone to Texas to find their father, playing on the one thing they had in common—Grayson's deceased wife. Kate and Rebecca had grown up together on this ranch.

No one was fool enough to think that buying the Trails West Ranch in Montana hadn't been Kate's idea. The ranch had been in her family for decades, until her father died and it was lost.

"Kate isn't the only one with history here," Russell argued. "Let's not forget that our mother was born and raised here." Rebecca Wade's father had been the foreman of the ranch. She and Kate had been like sisters. "This place means a lot to both Dad and Kate and should to all of us, as well."

"We're doing this for Dad," Russell continued. "And Mom. It's what she wanted."

Shane shook his head as he watched Russell step over to the bar, pick up the knife their father had used to slice up limes for margaritas, and proceed to cut five straws into five different lengths.

Taking another drink, Shane swore under his breath as a hush fell over the room. He couldn't believe they were really going to do this.

Russell mixed up the pieces in his hand, leveling off the cut straws at the top, hiding their lengths in his massive fist.

"This is crazy," Lantry said, looking to Shane for help. Shane knew that he was considered the sensible brother. After all, he was the Texas Ranger. Or at least had been.

Russell held out the cut straws. "Who wants to go first?"

"Not me," Jud said quickly. "I'm leaving mine up to destiny. I'll take the last straw."

"Hell, I'll go first," Dalton said, and drew one, palming it until the others had drawn.

Lantry went next, although he didn't seem any happier about it than Shane. Part con artist and charmer—if there was a way out of this, Lantry, the lawyer would find it.

"Shane?" Russell held his closed fist out to him.

"I don't want any part of this," Shane said with a curse.

"If you get the longest straw, you have five years before you have to do anything," Russell said, always the pragmatist. "By then Dad may be gone, too. You can ignore both of their dying wishes and do whatever the hell you please. In the meantime, take a damned straw."

Shane snatched one of the cut straws from his brother's hand, tossed it on the table without looking at it and poured himself another drink.

"You lucky bastard," Dalton said. "Shane got the longest one."

Russell turned to the youngest of the brothers. "Well, Jud, you still sure you want to go last?"

Jud stared down at the tops of the two remaining straws. "Yeah."

Russell drew one, and Jud took the only remaining straw.

"Okay, let's get this over with," Lantry said. He held out his straw to compare it to the others.

Shane was the only one who didn't join in. As he took a drink, he heard Jud swear and smiled to himself. The youngest of them had drawn the shortest straw. Maybe there was something to this karma business after all.

"Can't argue with destiny, Jud," he said. His brother collapsed into a chair beside him to brood or, more than likely, try to figure out an angle to get out of this. The brothers all had that in common—they all looked for a way out of whatever situation they found themselves in.

Shane had gotten the longest straw. Not that it mattered. This whole thing was ludicrous, and he wasn't going to be blackmailed into anything—especially marriage.

"Okay," Russell said. "Jud, you have one year in which to find a suitable wife. Lantry is next, then Dalton, me and Shane."

"I say we do it over. Best two out of three," Jud suggested. All four brothers turned on him. "Okay, okay. I suppose it's time I started thinking about settling down."

They all laughed. Of the five of them, Jud was the wildest when it came to horses—and women. The Hollywood stuntman settle down with one woman anytime soon? Not likely. On every film he was involved in, he usually had a couple of girlfriends.

"I told you this wasn't going to work," Shane said. "It's not the way to find a woman to spend the rest of your life with."

"Come on, none of us would marry unless forced to," Lantry said with a laugh. "Look at Dad. After Mom's death, he had all kinds of chances to marry, and he didn't."

"Not till Kate," Jud said.

"Maybe Kate reminds him of our mother," Dalton said.

Russell shook his head. "Kate is nothing like our mother." As the oldest at thirty-two, Russell had the best memory of their mother. "Anyway, Dad always said there was no one like Mom."

Shane said nothing. He'd only been around Kate at the wedding, but there was something about her that had made him suspicious, even before she talked their father into selling his place in Texas and moving to this isolated part of Montana to buy back her family's home ranch.

Kate was a woman with secrets. Shane had been a lawman for too long not to recognize it. Kate was hiding something. Something big. And Shane feared that when the truth came out, Grayson Corbett would be devastated.

"I'll have you know that I've already found the perfect woman," Jud announced. "Her name is Maddie Cavanaugh. She's exactly what mother said she wanted for us—a Montana girl."

The rest of them laughed, but Shane watched his little brother, thinking he might actually be telling the truth. Jud did attract women the way magnets attracted tacks. And Jud had been in town for over a week now.

"Dad and Kate are going to love Maddie," Jud said with a grin. "I predict wedding bells in the very near future."

Shane got to his feet. He couldn't take any more of this. "Have you all lost your minds? Who gives a damn what's in some stupid letter? Our mother didn't live long enough to know any of us well enough to determine what kind of woman we should marry. Why should we let her tell us how to live our lives from the grave?" He shook his head.

JERILYN DROVE as far as she could. She'd been running on fear and large doses of caffeine. Now after fifteen hours at the wheel her nerves were fried and she had the jitters so bad she was forced to stop for what was left of the night.

She pulled over beside a park in some small town and climbed into the back of the car to sleep, telling herself that she'd put enough miles between her and Earl Ray. There was no way he could find her, especially without a car and without knowing which direction she was headed. She'd never told him about the daughter she'd been forced to give up at sixteen. She'd never told anyone.

And she was sure he hadn't called the cops. No, Earl Ray would call some of his low-life buddies and probably get drunk. That was his answer to everything.

It was when he sobered up that she would have to worry. Then he'd be hungover and furious. But why come looking for her at all? He could just pick up another down-on-her-luck woman at any bar. Those were the only kind of women who put up with Earl Ray.

Her stomach growled, but with gas being so expensive, she had gone without food. In the morning, though, she'd have to get something to eat. She had to take care of herself if she hoped to get to Montana.

As she curled up to sleep, she thought about her little baby girl. Jerilyn tried to picture what Maddie would look like now and hoped her daughter had blond hair and blue eyes just like her real mama.

Jerilyn wished she could get some new clothes before she met her and maybe even buy her daughter a gift. Flowers, maybe, or chocolates.

Her stomach growled again, and she tried to sleep, but every little sound startled her. Finally sometime before dawn, Jerilyn fell into a deep sleep and dreamed about her reunion with her daughter.

GRAYSON CORBETT stood at the window watching his wife. *His wife*. He smiled at the thought. Falling in love had come as a surprise.

He'd never thought there would be anyone but Rebecca. In all those years since her death, he never met a woman who stirred his heart or tempted him to remarry.

Until Kate.

She'd come into his life so late. That was his only regret. At fifty-five, he hated that he wouldn't have an entire lifetime with her. But if Rebecca had taught him anything, it was not to count on more than this moment in time.

He and Rebecca had married young and started a family right away. They'd both wanted lots of kids, but Grayson lost the love of his life right after the twins were born.

He'd never expected to love again.

As he studied Kate's slim back now, he ached at the sight of the way she hugged herself as she looked out across the land—her family's land.

He'd hoped getting her family ranch back would take away that haunted look he'd sometimes glimpsed in her eyes.

But there was more to her sadness than the loss of mere land. Something powerful had a hold on her. Whatever it was, Kate kept it to herself.

Grayson hoped he could gain her trust and that she would open up to him. So far that hadn't happened.

"Dad?"

Grayson turned to find his youngest son standing in the doorway. He motioned Jud in, smiling in spite of himself. Having his sons all under the same roof again, even for a short period of time, brought him more joy than they could imagine.

"I thought you'd want to know we talked and came to a decision," Jud said.

Grayson held his breath, worried that his foolish plan hadn't worked. He was torn between guilt and hope.

"We drew straws," Jud said.

So like his sons. He smiled. "Straws, huh? How did you come out?"

Jud shook his head, grinning. "Wouldn't you know it? I got the shortest."

"What do you plan to do?"

"What choice do I have?"

Grayson hated forcing his sons into this, but if he hoped to live long enough to see grandchildren, what choice did he have?

"Think of it as a nudge," he'd told Kate when he'd revealed his plan to her after finding the letter.

"Oh, Grayson," she'd said, looking worried. "Are you sure about this?"

Hell, no. But he knew his sons too well. Threats and bribes wouldn't have worked. All five sons were successful, and telling them they'd lose their inheritance if they didn't marry wouldn't work. Making an old-man's plea to them wouldn't have worked, either.

He'd raised strong-willed, highly independent men. They were all more like him than Rebecca.

It wasn't until he found the letters Rebecca had left to be given to each son on his wedding day that Grayson seized on the idea. For years, he hadn't touched anything of Rebecca's. Not until the move to Montana. He'd been shocked to find the letters—and grateful. Rebecca, even from the grave, had helped him decide what to do about their wild, incorrigible sons.

Along with a letter to each of the boys, Rebecca had

left him a letter, as well. In it, her dying wish had been that the boys marry before the age of thirty-five. She half jokingly had said she hoped that they would marry a Montana cowgirl—just as their father had.

"Don't look so guilty," Kate said when he'd told her he'd called the boys to Montana for a family meeting. "You only want the best for your sons."

Grayson hadn't been so sure. He'd felt as if he was being selfish by using Rebecca's dying wish.

"Honey," Kate had said. "Your boys are like you, strong—stubborn and independent to a fault."

He knew she was right. The boys had grown up without a mother and in a house without a woman's touch. They'd seen him live for years without the love of a good woman and with everything on his own terms.

But since he'd fallen for Kate, he'd come to realize how important love and marriage were for a man. He wanted the same for his sons, and he wanted his sons to settle in Montana, close enough that they could be a family again.

"How are they taking all of this?" Grayson asked his son.

Jud laughed. "As expected."

He laughed, as well. "I can just imagine." Russell would take command as the oldest. Lantry would look for a loophole. Shane would rebel. Dalton would try to charm his way out of it. And Jud…

Grayson studied his youngest son. The wildest one. What would Jud do?

A TRAIL OF DUST rose on the horizon. Kate Wade Corbett watched the three riders cut across the wide prairie.

The Corbett brothers were racing each other to the corrals. Competition was in their blood.

All five brothers were so much like Grayson. No wonder none of them wanted to settle down. She hoped that her husband's plan worked, but she couldn't help being doubtful.

"Hello."

Kate smiled as he felt Grayson's warm breath on her neck. As he put his arms around her, she leaned back into him and breathed in his masculine scent.

"The boys drew straws to see who would get married first," Grayson whispered.

Boys. He still thought of them as boys, but they were grown men. Too bad they often didn't act like it, she thought as dust billowed up, and the breeze carried their shouts and laughter.

"Jud got the shortest straw," he said. "He says he's met someone he thinks we'll like."

She sighed and chuckled softly. "And you believe him?"

"Still skeptical, huh?"

Kate turned in his arms to cup his smooth-shaven jaw and look into those incredible blue eyes. "Wouldn't it have been easier just to tell them the truth?"

He shook his head, smiling down at her before gently giving her a kiss. "I just want them to be as happy as I am," he said as they turned to watch the finish of the race.

In a cloud of dust and cheers and curses, Dalton reached the corrals first. Lantry and Russell finished neck and neck. As the dust settled, Kate spotted Shane sitting in the shade of the bunkhouse. She hadn't noticed him before, but she now had the distinct feeling that he'd been watching her and his father.

Shane, she feared, saw more than the others. Of the five, he worried her the most.

Chapter Three

Jud Corbett wasn't about to tell his brothers, but he'd known this was coming. He was working on a film just to the north in Canada and had overheard Kate and his father discussing the family meeting on one of his visits.

At first he'd told himself that his brothers wouldn't go along with any crazy marriage pact, but that was before he heard about the letters from their mother. While none of the brothers would want to disappoint the old man, ignoring wishes of the mother they'd heard about their whole lives would be impossible.

Jud had known that this whole situation would be a train wreck. That was why he had immediately started looking for the perfect girl-next-door to bring home. He knew his father and Kate would only approve of a woman unlike the kind he normally dated.

He'd found her on a local online dating service's Web site. The moment he'd seen Maddie Cavanaugh's face, he'd known she was perfect.

Imagine his disappointment when he'd found out that the woman's photo and personal profile had been put up on the site by accident. According to Arlene Evans, who ran the service, Maddie Cavanaugh wasn't even in the area anymore.

But a few days ago, Jud had seen Maddie coming out of the Whitehorse Drugstore. Her photo on the Web site hadn't done her justice.

Her long blond hair was pulled up in a ponytail. A pair of silver loops dangled from each earlobe. She wore no makeup. Freckles were sprinkled across her cheeks and the bridge of her nose like tiny stars in a Montana night sky.

Her slim figure was clad in a Western shirt, jeans and boots, which looked at home on her. She had pushed her sunglasses up into her hair to glance down at the book she was holding. When she raised her head, she'd looked right at him with a pair of wondrous big blue eyes, which held an innocence that took his breath away.

Jud was within a few feet of her when she glanced at her watch and then took off toward her pickup, which was parked across the street. He watched her go, chuckling to himself.

He knew he was considered the wildest of the Corbett brothers. Earning his reputation had taken hard work since his four older brothers had sown more than their share of wild oats.

But as he stared after Maddie Cavanaugh, Jud knew he had found the perfect bride.

AT A GAS STATION on her way north, Jerilyn was in the process of digging in her large shoulder bag, looking for what was left of Earl Ray's money when she found it.

"What's this?" Frowning, she pulled out a small black notebook. The leather was worn, and she gingerly peeked between the covers, wondering how it had gotten into her bag.

Inside were names, numbers and dates. Her stomach roiled as she recognized some of the names, names from the news. She dropped the book onto the car seat as if the pages had scorched her fingers and covered her mouth to keep from screaming.

For a few minutes, Jerilyn couldn't think, couldn't do anything but panic. While she had no idea what exactly the names and numbers meant, she had to get this book back to Earl Ray.

Otherwise…

She swallowed and looked down the long highway she'd just driven and reassured herself that Earl Ray didn't have a clue where she was going.

She knew, now more than ever, that he wouldn't go to the cops because they were the last people he wanted seeing this little notebook. No, the book was worth much more to those members of organized crime who'd been in the news. This book would put them behind bars for life. No wonder she and Earl Ray had been living in dumpy motels under assumed names for weeks.

She hadn't believed him when he kept saying his ship was about to come in and that they'd be eating lobster tail and living in penthouses.

But now that she'd found this book, she realized Earl Ray had just been waiting around for the right buyer. How had he gotten his hands on this?

Jerilyn felt herself growing calmer as she realized

that she not only had something that Earl Ray wanted—she had something worth a bunch of money. This book could be her backup plan. If things didn't work out with Maddie's family, she could always make a deal with Earl Ray.

Of course, any negotiations with Earl Ray would be dangerous—much more dangerous than meeting her daughter's family and convincing them to help her financially.

Jerilyn tucked the book back into her bag. Once she got to Montana, she'd have to find a safe place to hide it until she decided what to do.

MADDIE WAS LATE. It wasn't the first time and wouldn't be the last. She'd picked up a novel in the drugstore, started reading and couldn't put it down. The next thing she knew she'd lost track of time.

As she sped down the street toward the restaurant, she hoped her cousin Laci wouldn't be angry with her. Maddie felt terrible about being late to her own welcome-home party. She'd stopped by the drugstore to buy a nice card to thank Laci for throwing her the party and ended up in the fiction section. She should have known better.

When she pulled up across the street from Northern Lights, the restaurant co-owned by Laci and her husband, Bridger Duvall, she saw all the cars.

She felt a wave of panic. All of her friends and neighbors and family from around Whitehorse were here. These people all knew about her broken engagement to Bo Evans, and for a moment Maddie thought about driving on past. How could she face everyone?

For years now, she'd been away at college and had avoided coming back. But she'd missed her cousins Laci and Laney, along with this part of Montana. Not to mention her horse, which her cousins had been boarding for her.

Maddie wished she'd never agreed to this party, though. But Laci was very persuasive; she loved cooking and throwing parties. As Maddie pulled into a parking spot, she tried to talk herself out of running away.

Just then Laney appeared at her side window. One look in her cousin's eyes and Maddie saw that she understood her fears.

Maddie cut the engine and rolled down the window. "I'm such a coward."

"No, you're not," Laney said, giving her a sympathetic smile. "All those people in there have missed you. They love you, Maddie, and are so excited to have you home."

Maddie's eyes brimmed with tears as her cousin opened the pickup door.

"Laci and I will be right there with you. I promise you will have a good time."

Maddie nodded and bolstered her courage by reminding herself that Bo Evans had left town. She knew, though, that he wasn't the only reason she hadn't returned for so long. No, the real reason she'd fled Old Town Whitehorse was a secret she prayed would never come out.

JUD KNEW he had to act quickly. His brothers could stand around arguing about their mother's motives for forcing marriage on them, but it seemed pretty transparent to Jud that the old man wanted his sons to settle in Montana or he would have never told them about the letters.

If there were even any letters left from their mother to be read on each of their wedding days. Maybe her dying wish really hadn't been that her sons find wives.

None of that really mattered to Jud.

He was doing this for his father. Come hell or high water, Jud intended to give the old man what he wanted—a wedding. Just not the wedding everyone was expecting.

In a town the size of Whitehorse, it didn't take Jud but a matter of minutes to find out where Maddie Cavanaugh had gone. Crashing the welcome-home party had been child's play, since most everyone in town had been invited.

Seeing her again reinforced his belief that she was exactly what he was looking for, and yet he hesitated. Unlike the other women he'd been with, Maddie didn't have obvious sexual appeal. She was understated. That's what she was. Sweet-looking. Real.

She was also completely wrong for him, and he suspected she would know it soon enough.

He'd known even before he reached her that she would turn him down for a date. He would have been disappointed if she hadn't.

"Maybe some other time," he'd said, looking regretful as he backed off. But as he left, he saw out of the corner of his eye that she was watching him leave. Her cousins were at her side, whispering something to her. No doubt encouraging her.

Smiling to himself, he left, betting himself he'd have a date with her before the day was out.

Maddie Cavanaugh wasn't getting away. Too much was at stake here.

"So TELL US about this Maddie Cavanaugh," Lantry said at breakfast several mornings later.

Jud grinned. He was going out for lunch with Maddie and planned to take her to the theatre in town tonight. But while he had to return to his film in Canada tomorrow, he had another date with her to the rodeo the day after. "You'll see for yourself when you meet her."

"We've been waiting to meet her," Lantry said. "Come on, fess up, there isn't any Maddie Cavanaugh. You made her up, thinking it would buy you time."

"I couldn't make up a woman like Maddie," Jud said in all seriousness, then concentrated on his breakfast. Juanita had served huevos rancheros with homemade tortillas and beans, his favorite.

"So when are you going to bring her out to meet Dad and Kate?" Dalton asked from the end of the table. "Or isn't that Hollywood charm of yours working?"

"All in good time," Jud said. "When you're serious about a woman you need to take things slow. You'll learn that if you ever date a woman more than once."

Lantry cocked his head at his brother and narrowed his eyes. "You've never been secretive about any of the women you were dating. Quite the contrary. You're up to something."

"Just true love," Jud said with a grin.

TWO DAYS LATER, Shane had his feet propped up on the porch railing and his hat pulled down low against the afternoon sun. He appeared to be asleep, but Grayson knew better.

"You still planning to go back to the Texas Rangers?" he asked quietly.

Shane didn't stir. "Why wouldn't I?"

Grayson suspected his son's wounds ran much deeper than the gunshot wound he'd suffered a month ago. "Montana could use a good lawman."

Shane chuckled and pushed back his Stetson to look at his father. "Subtle."

"Kate says I need to be more direct."

"You're plenty direct the way you are," he said, sitting up.

Grayson smiled. "I get the feeling you're ticked off at me."

"You think?"

"What's wrong with wanting my family close by?"

"You're the one who moved to Montana."

"You goin' to hold that against me?"

Shane sighed. "What's going on, Dad? It isn't like you to sell lock, stock and barrel and leave Texas the way you did."

Grayson shook his head. "Love changes everything, son. I hope you find that out for yourself one day."

"No, thanks. Not if it makes me change everything about myself."

"Is that what you think happened to me?"

"You've got to admit this letter thing is beneath you."

Grayson leaned back his chair and stared out across

the summer-green prairie. This land, with its rolling grassland that ran to coulees filled with juniper and scrub pine and rocky outcroppings before dropping into the Missouri River gorge, had drawn him the first time he'd seen it.

He loved the sweet summer scents, loved the way the place was steeped in history, loved riding across the great expanse of country, the grasses, tall and green, undulating in the breeze.

But mostly he loved this place because it had once been Kate's and was now hers again. He'd given her the ranch, but it was so little compared to what she'd given him. His heart swelled at the mere thought of his wife.

But his marriage and this move had put more than miles between him and his sons. He couldn't bear the thought that he might lose them because of it.

"It's selfish of me," he said to Shane. "To want to uproot you boys to make an old man happy."

Shane laughed. "Blackmail first, now guilt?" He shook his head. "Hell, why don't you pull out all the stops and tell us you're—" Shane stopped as if the word *dying* had caught in his throat. Swallowing, he said, "Does this really mean that much to you?"

"Yes," Grayson said, meeting his son's gaze and holding it. "It means that much to me."

Shane looked into his father's eyes, his pulse drumming in his ears. His next breath came hard as he realized he might have stumbled onto the truth. "You aren't…sick, are you?"

He couldn't bring himself to say the *D* word. He'd

come too close to saying it only moments before. Grayson looked as healthy as a horse, but there was no denying he'd aged. His hair had grayed and there were deep lines furrowing his brow.

"I'm fine," Grayson said and looked away. "I don't want you to feel…"

"Trapped?"

"No." His father's gaze came back to him, his eyes shiny. "I raised you boys to be your own men. I would never want to do anything to change that."

Shane swore under his breath. He'd told himself his father wasn't going to make him feel guilty about not going along with this stupid marriage pact, and yet he felt guilty as hell right now.

The phone rang inside the house. Neither man moved. After the second ring, Juanita picked up. Shane could hear her and knew even before she stepped to the porch doorway that the call was for him.

"It's Jud," she said, handing him the phone. "He says it's urgent."

KATE HAD been into the town of Whitehorse as few times as possible since her return to Montana. She'd let Juanita take care of the shopping and was happy to stay out at the ranch, venturing out only to ride the property and marvel at how fortunate she was to have a man like Grayson Corbett in love with her.

But she couldn't keep making excuses for avoiding town without someone getting suspicious. So she'd started venturing in a few times, making the trips short.

She knew that she'd eventually come face-to-face with her past.

Today she'd gone into the hardware store to pick up an extension cord, and as she came out she practically ran into a tall, slim, older cowboy waiting on the sidewalk.

Even after all these years, Chester Bailey hadn't changed much. He was still a good-looking man. His blond hair was graying at the temples and there were lines around his blue eyes, but she had no problem recognizing him.

"Kate?" He sounded incredulous. *"Kate Wade?"*

"It's Corbett now," she said. "Hello, Chester."

He stared at her, shaking his head as if he couldn't believe his eyes. "I heard someone had bought your folks' ranch…Corbett." He smiled. "So that's you."

She nodded. "How have you been?"

"Good. I suppose you heard. Lila and I are divorced."

She hadn't heard because until recently she'd made a point of putting Whitehorse behind her. "I'm sorry," she said. "You were married a long time."

He nodded, head dipping. "Over thirty years."

Kate felt all those old emotions stir inside her and wished she'd never come to town. Never come back here. As she stood there, she was afraid of what she would say next and terrified of what Chester might reply.

Fortunately, she didn't have to worry. A middle-aged woman came out of the local clothing store, laughing with a friend. She and the friend parted company, and the woman headed toward Chester.

Kate saw at once that this was who Chester had been

waiting for. The blonde was younger than Chester, her hair short and curly, her smile coming easily.

"Hi," Kate said, as the woman took Chester's arm. She noted that the woman wasn't wearing a wedding ring. A girlfriend?

"Susie, this is Kate…Corbett."

Susie's face brightened. "Corbett? You bought the old Trails West Ranch. I've always admired that place. I'm so glad someone is living there again."

Kate waited for Chester to tell his girlfriend that the ranch used to belong to Kate's family, that she'd grown up here, that the two of them had known each other.

When Chester told his girlfriend none of that, Kate said, "Thank you."

"Well, welcome to Whitehorse," Susie said. "You're going to love it here. Everyone is so friendly. Stop by the Hi-Line Café. Chester and I own the place."

"Best chicken-fried steak in town," Chester said, seeming a little embarrassed, since it was clear that he'd never told his girlfriend about Kate. Nor, apparently, was he going to.

"I'll do that sometime," Kate said. She took a step backward, relieved for the chance to escape.

She walked briskly to her SUV and sat behind the wheel, trying to quit shaking. Seeing Chester had brought it all back.

Why had she let Grayson move them here? She'd been shocked when he'd told her about her present on their one-month anniversary.

"I bought you something," he'd said, seeming shy and excited.

She'd laughed. "Whatever it is, I know I'm going to love it."

"Well, you used to love it."

Her heart had begun to pound even before he said the words: "I bought you Trails West."

She'd realized her mistake at once. From the first day when she'd shown up at Grayson's Texas ranch, he'd wanted to hear all about the years she'd lived in Montana. She'd told him what it was like growing up with Rebecca and how they'd been close as sisters until Rebecca went to college in Texas, where she met and married him.

Kate had also told Grayson about her father's death and losing the ranch. What she hadn't told him was the rest of it.

"Grayson, you shouldn't have," she'd said, unable to hold back the tears as he handed her the deed to the ranch.

He'd thought they were tears of joy, and he had been so happy to give her the ranch that she couldn't tell him it was the last thing she wanted.

Her second shock had come a few months later, when he'd surprised her with the news that he'd bought up property around Trails West and was selling out in Texas. Grayson didn't do anything halfway. It was why he'd been so successful.

"I love the country up there, so I'm not doing this just for you," he'd told her.

Kate knew that his sons believed she'd talked him into moving to Montana and blamed her. She was at fault, no doubt about that. She should have spoken up right away and put an end to this before it got completely out of hand.

But she loved Grayson too much.

And she had to admit it was great being back on the ranch. All the wonderful memories of her father and her childhood were here.

Grayson loved hearing about her memories of life on the ranch with Rebecca. She knew it helped give Rebecca a new life for him. Surprisingly, it seemed to free him, as well. He suddenly felt ready to finally go through Rebecca's things. That's when they'd found the letters Rebecca had left for her sons.

As Kate started the SUV, wanting nothing more than to return to the ranch and Grayson, her heart swelled as she thought about his capacity for love. She didn't deserve him. She didn't deserve any of this, she thought as she drove out of Whitehorse.

Her life was a fairy tale, perfect in every way. Except for one—Chester Bailey and the lie between them. When Grayson learned the truth, she feared her fairy tale would turn into a nightmare.

Chapter Four

After Jud's "urgent" call, Shane hooked up the horse trailer, cursing the whole while. As he climbed into the cab of the truck, he realized he was winded. He told himself it was from anger at his brother for roping him into babysitting Jud's girlfriend.

But there was no denying the truth. It was from this small amount of exertion, which meant he'd only been kidding himself about being ready to go back to his job as a Texas Ranger—and this scared him more than he wanted to admit.

He'd expected to bounce right back. It wasn't like it was the first time he'd been shot. He'd tried to tell himself that this time was no different.

"Like hell," he grumbled, as he started the pickup. Every night since the shooting, he'd relived it in his nightmares. This time wasn't just different. This time had changed everything. The mere thought of not being able to go back made him furious, especially after all the years he'd worked toward becoming a Texas Ranger.

He quickly turned his anger back to Jud, not wanting

to deal with the other issue. He feared it wasn't being shot that was the problem. Something was missing, and he knew he wasn't in the right frame of mind to even consider what that something might be.

"I'm in a terrible bind," Jud had said when he'd called from the set of his latest movie. "Shooting has run over and I promised Maddie—"

"Maddie? This woman you just met? I'm sure she'll understand."

"She can't round up another horse trailer at this late notice," Jud argued. "Hers is in the shop, and the rodeo is in a few hours."

"Nice that you waited until the last minute."

"I'd hoped I could get out of here and not let her down."

Shane fought to curb his temper. He didn't want to get involved in this little love affair Jud had going with a local girl. If that's what it was. The family had yet to meet her—and Jud was acting odder than usual. In fact, Lantry was convinced the woman didn't even exist, and that Jud was up to something other than romance.

Shane tended to agree with Lantry. It wasn't like Jud not to talk about the woman he was dating. Jud was probably just humoring their father, making it look as if he was keeping up his end of the marriage pact. Even if this woman existed, Shane didn't believe for a moment that Jud had any intention of marrying her.

Because of that, going to pick her up made him more than a little uncomfortable. Shane didn't want to be within a hundred miles when Jud broke this poor young woman's heart.

"Just tell me where I need to go," Shane had finally said. He was angry with his brother, but he felt he needed to meet this woman and decide for himself what his brother was up to.

"She's staying with her cousins on a ranch outside of Old Town Whitehorse. I owe you, Shane. I really appreciate this."

Right, Shane thought, as he drove out of the Trails West Ranch, dust billowing up behind his pickup and horse trailer.

It crossed his mind that standing up Maddie Cavanaugh might be Jud's way of letting her down easily. If so, Shane would wring his brother's neck when he saw him.

The land stretched out to the horizon, golden in the afternoon sun. Shane had seen some of the country when he'd driven up from Texas. To the south was the rugged terrain of the Breaks, where the Missouri River cut a gorge through the plains on its way to the Mississippi, the Louisiana delta and finally the Gulf of Mexico.

The Breaks had been home to many an outlaw in Montana's past, the miles of wilderness providing hideouts along the river. Butch Cassidy and the Sundance Kid had allegedly robbed a train outside of Whitehorse before taking off for South America.

Maybe his father hadn't been foolish to buy a ranch up here. But the fact that the ranch had belonged to Kate's family still bothered Shane. Plus, the Trails West Ranch was to hell and gone, south of Whitehorse near the Breaks, out in the middle of nowhere. The closest airport and real city were a good three hours away.

Grayson couldn't have moved farther away from Texas without leaving the country. At least he'd stayed in the lower forty-eight. Shane guessed he should be thankful for that.

Fortunately, Grayson and Kate had talked Juanita into moving up with them, so at least the food was familiar—Tex-Mex, homemade tortillas every morning and barbecued brisket and Texas beans on warm evenings.

Shane was also thankful for a place to recuperate. If truth be told, he'd wanted out of Texas for a while. The memories of his ordeal had ridden shotgun with him the whole trip, but it was easier here, easier to worry about his father and Kate and this stupid marriage pact than to face what he'd left in Texas. Or was it lost in Texas—what he may have *lost* in Texas—being able to return as a Ranger.

Once Shane hit the main highway, he wound his way north to town. Whitehorse was small and Western, all pickups and cowboy hats and boots. A dozen trucks were parked along Main Street, the town bustling because of the Whitehorse Days celebration.

He turned on the radio and got drumming on the Native American station. It made him think of yesterday, when the daily polka came on the radio. Kate and his father danced around the kitchen, laughing and kicking up their heels. The sight had left a lump in his throat.

How could he be suspicious of Kate when she clearly made his father so happy? Sometimes he hated the lawman in himself.

Whitehorse was so small it was easy to run out of town. Shane quickly found himself in the country again. The road turned to gravel, the country dotted with cattle. Five miles later, he spotted a sign for Old Town Whitehorse barely sticking up out of the tall grass.

The first settlement of Whitehorse had been nearer the Missouri River, but when the railroad came through, the town migrated north, taking the name with it.

Locals now referred to the original settlement as Old Town Whitehorse. These days it was little more than a ghost town.

At one time, there'd been a gas station but that building was sitting empty, the pumps long gone. There was a community center—every ranching community up here had one—and a one-room schoolhouse that still looked as if it was being used.

Past that, there were a few houses. One large one was boarded up and had a Condemned sign nailed to the door.

As Shane kept going, he circled around what was left of the town and headed west. He hadn't gone far when he saw the sign to the Cavanaugh place. Jud had told him that Maddie was staying with her great-aunt and uncle, Titus and Pearl Cavanaugh, both descendents of early homesteaders.

Titus was as close to a mayor as Old Town Whitehorse had. He provided a church service every Sunday morning at the community center and saw to the hiring of a schoolteacher when needed.

Pearl, who was recovering from a stroke, was involved with the Whitehorse Sewing Circle, which her mother and her husband's had started years ago. The women of the community still got together to make quilts for every new baby and every newlywed in the area.

Jud had provided more information than Shane had wanted or needed to hear. He just wanted to see Maddie for himself and make up his own mind. Then he planned to stay as far away from Jud's affairs as possible—just as he'd always done.

Shane told himself that once he got Maddie and her horse to the fairgrounds, he'd leave the horse trailer, go back to the ranch and not give Maddie another thought. Jud had promised to make it down in time to drive Maddie and her horse home from the rodeo.

As Shane parked and walked toward the Cavanaugh house, he spotted a blond cowgirl waiting on the front porch. He was instantly taken aback. Was this Maddie Cavanaugh? If so, then she was nothing like the women Jud dated.

She was cute enough—curvy but slim, blond and blue-eyed. She had a fresh-faced innocence about her. Maybe it was the freckles. Or the wide blue eyes. She just looked too damned sweet for Jud's tastes.

Shane noticed that she was dressed in jeans, boots and a blue-checked shirt. Her long blond hair was plaited in a single braid that snaked out from under her Western straw hat. She apparently was waiting for him. He gave her points for that. There was nothing he disliked more than a woman who made a man wait just because she could.

"Maddie?"

She nodded and smiled.

"I'm Shane. Jud's brother."

He'd half-expected her to be in a snit since Jud had stood her up, but she didn't seem upset in the least as he headed up the steps toward her. If anything, she looked curious. Was it possible Jud hadn't called to tell her of the change in plans?

"Jud couldn't make it," Shane said. "He sent me."

Maddie eyed him for a moment. "You should have just called. I could have gotten someone to take my horse in."

He knew he hadn't sounded very friendly. He'd sounded put out. He wanted to tell her that it wasn't her—that it was Jud and this stupid marriage pact and knowing this so-called relationship was going to end badly.

"I don't mind," Shane said, although clearly he did, and he could tell she knew it. "Ready?" Her eyes were a shade lighter than his own, piercing in a way that made him feel she could see right through him.

Maddie seemed to be making up her mind whether or not to let him take her into town.

He shoved back his hat and chewed at his cheek, wishing he could think of something to say. His brothers were the smooth talkers, not him.

After a few seconds, she rose, brushed off the seat of her jeans, not looking any happier about this than he was. "Since you came all this way, I'll get my horse."

Part of him wished she would just send him packing. But at the same time, he'd have felt badly. Shane hated feeling he was involved in Jud's deception.

After they loaded her horse, Maddie climbed into the pickup cab. He tried to think of something to say on the way into town, but fortunately, she seemed fine without talking.

She gazed out the window as if soaking up her surroundings. He recalled that Jud had said she'd been away and had only just returned.

"Did I tell you Jud got tied up with a movie?" he asked.

"He'd said he might."

So Jud had already set up his excuse to get out of this. Shane silently cursed his brother.

"That's my brother," he said, wishing he could bring himself to tell her about Jud and save her a lot of heartache. Feeling Maddie's gaze on him, he glanced in her direction and saw something in her blue eyes that surprised him.

Earlier her eyes had been in shadow under the brim of the Western hat she had snugged down over her blond hair. She'd seemed so young, so innocent, so downright naïve. He'd thought this freckle-faced cowgirl from a forgotten part of Montana was a sitting duck for just about any man. Especially Jud Corbett. But now he had a clear view as she met his gaze dead-on. What he saw in all that blue wasn't dewy-eyed innocence, though. There was intelligence there, and pain.

He had to reevaluate his first impression. Was it possible that Maddie couldn't be easily taken in by his Hollywood stuntman brother Jud?

For her sake, Shane certainly hoped so.

JERILYN HAD NEVER made New Years resolutions, planned for the future or worked toward a career.

Once her family money was gone, she depended on

whatever man she was with to take care of her. If she thought ahead at all, it was only to consider what to eat or drink within the next few minutes.

That was why she had a moment of uncertainty as she drove into Whitehorse. She realized she lacked a plan and she didn't have a clue how to find her daughter.

On the way into town, she drove under a banner that read: *Welcome to Whitehorse Days.*

Apparently it was a rodeo.

She drove through town, a little surprised at how small it was. The bars seemed to be hopping. A dozen pickups lined the main street, and everyone seemed to be dressed in Western attire.

Was it possible that the couple who had adopted her baby were ranchers? She liked the idea of a huge ranch and lots of cattle.

Her mother had sworn the baby had gone to a good family. That meant wealth in Jerilyn's mind, but what if she was wrong? What if Maddie's folks couldn't help her?

Jerilyn parked in front of a bar and sat for a moment, wishing Earl Ray was here with her. At least he'd know what to do next. Now she felt lost, afraid and alone. More and more, Jerilyn realized taking off on her own had been a mistake.

The neon of the bar lights flashed across the cracked windshield of Earl Ray's old Buick. Jerilyn couldn't believe the car had made it this far. But now she was broke, the engine was making a loud noise and a light on the dashboard had been blinking for the past twenty miles or so.

She'd ignored it, just hoping the car would get her to Whitehorse. Now here she was, sitting in the dark, cold and tired, and thinking she might have acted a little impulsively.

The bar door opened. A man came out, bringing with him the sound of music and laughter. Past his dark silhouette, she caught sight of the brightly lit bottles lined up behind the bar and a few patrons who were sitting on the bar stools.

That glimpse inside the bar drew Jerilyn with a familiar tug. Pulling the keys, she climbed out and headed toward the flashing bar lights.

As she opened the glass-front door, she saw her reflection. The bar better be dark, she thought, since she didn't look her best after so many hours in the car.

She smoothed a hand over her long, straight blond hair, bit her lips to give them a little color and stepped in.

The jukebox cranked out a familiar country-and-western tune, and the smell of stale beer wafted toward her like a welcoming committee. Jerilyn took it all in, the music, the smells, the crowded room.

She could almost taste the cold beer she was on the verge of ordering. Feeling as if she'd come home, Jerilyn sauntered over to the bar and slid her narrow behind up onto a stool.

Leaning her skinny arms on the cool, slick surface of the bar, she smiled at the middle-aged, balding bartender and ordered herself a bottle of light beer. As he dug in the cooler, she glanced at the four men lined up on the bar stools and gave them a look that was universal at every bar she'd ever been in.

The bartender put down a cocktail napkin and a cold glass to go with her bottle of beer. She took her time pouring the beer into the glass and then, closing her eyes, she drank in the cold, familiar brew and let out a contented sigh.

She'd had only two gulps of her beer before one of the men told the bartender to give her another. She tilted her glass in the man's direction, smiling her thanks.

By the time the bartender set a fresh bottle in front of her, the man had come down the bar to take the stool next to hers. It was like a dance, and Jerilyn knew the steps by heart.

Everything is going to be all right now, she told herself, as she smiled over at him.

Jerilyn took a sip of her beer, licked the foam from her lips and asked, "So are you from around here?"

SHANE HADN'T PLANNED on it, but he ended up staying for the rodeo. It wasn't like he had anything else to do. In truth, he was curious about Maddie. He wanted to see her ride. According to the program, she was entered in the women's barrel-racing event.

He knew he shouldn't have been surprised, but she was damned good on a horse. Maybe Maddie and Jud had more in common than he'd first thought. Jud was a trick rider and did a lot of Westerns along with his other stunt work. He loved horses, and it was clear that Maddie did, as well.

"I didn't know the Cavanaugh girl was back in town," said a woman who was seated in front of Shane on the bleachers. "I hope it's not because of that awful Bo Evans."

Shane couldn't help but wonder who Bo Evans was as he watched the next young woman ride.

The other rider came in with a slightly better time than Maddie. Shane was disappointed and knew Maddie must be, too. When the bucking-horse portion of the rodeo began, he decided to stay a little longer. He hadn't been to a rodeo in years. The smell of hot dogs, burgers and traveling tacos rose up to the stands where he was sitting. In the stalls, wild horses kicked up dust under the lights. Darkness lurked beyond, and he found himself lulled by the sound of the announcer's voice and the hooting and hollering of the crowd.

Rodeos and cowboys, it seemed, were the same all over the country. Shane felt strangely at home, even though he didn't know a soul in the whole place except for Maddie Cavanaugh, who was now talking with some of the other cowgirls.

As if she felt him looking at her, she turned, her gaze moving over the crowd on the bleachers until she found him.

He tried to look away, but her eyes held his, and he felt his heart kick up a beat, no doubt from being caught watching her.

She looked surprised to see him. Probably because he'd made it pretty clear he would be leaving as soon as he dropped off her and her horse.

Shane mentally kicked himself for being such a jackass. As she wandered off with her friends, he turned his attention back to the wild horse race, which was so chaotic and absorbing that he didn't even notice Jud sit down next to him until the event was almost over.

"Hey, this is some race," Shane said and then re-membered he was angry at his brother. "So you made it."

"Got out earlier than I'd thought. I'm surprised you stayed for the rodeo." Jud was studying him. "Did you think I was going to stand up Maddie and make you bail me out again?"

The thought had crossed Shane's mind. "She said she'd find a ride if you didn't make it."

Jud smiled. "Yeah, she's pretty independent. Part of her charm. So what do you think of her?"

Shane just shrugged as the wild horse race ended and a band nearby struck up a boot-stomping song.

Jud grinned over at him. "I think she's amazing, a real Montana cowgirl and just about the prettiest little thing. But she's got some backbone, too. I like that about her."

Shane had to bite his tongue. Maddie seemed like a nice young woman who deserved better than his Romeo brother. For a moment, he concentrated on watching the riders rounding up the wild horses, then rose. No reason to stay any longer.

"I need to find Maddie and tell her I'm here," Jud said. "If you see her on your way out, would you tell her I'm looking for her?"

"Yeah, sure." His intention had been to get the hell out of there, but the crowd moved in the direction of the music, and Shane found himself caught up in it. He couldn't remember the last time he'd been to an outdoor dance and found himself drawn to the country-and-western music being cranked out by the band.

Maddie was standing at the edge of the makeshift dance floor. She was tapping her toe to the song, looking like a woman who wanted to dance. Shane was glad Jud had at least made it in time for this.

He hesitated about giving her Jud's message. Then, feeling foolish, he told himself it was the least he could do, since he hadn't been very nice to her earlier. Maybe he'd even compliment her on her ride.

As he neared, the lights strung through the trees glittered above her head, and her upturned face glowed. Her Western straw hat was pushed back; her blond hair now splayed loose around her shoulders.

She seemed to be watching the other dancers and enjoying herself. Shane was almost to her when she suddenly tensed. All the joy washed away, her freckles popping out as the blood seemed to drain from her face.

Shane quickly followed her gaze and saw a cowboy in a black hat push himself away from the flatbed truck being used as a portable beer garden and start toward her.

Maddie took a step back, eyes wide, glancing around as if searching for a place to hide.

Without thinking, Shane stepped in front of her, cutting off the cowboy who was almost to her.

"Dance," Shane said, taking Maddie's hand and pulling her to him as he swung her away from the cowboy and out onto the dance floor.

Shane felt her trembling, and the lights caught the disquiet in her eyes. He drew her protectively closer as he two-stepped her to the other side of the dance floor.

The cowboy was where they'd left him, glaring across at them.

"Who was that?" Shane asked.

"Nobody." She met his gaze, and he felt another tremor quake through her.

Instinctively, he drew her closer, wanting to protect her. She felt good in his arms, soft and very female. Shane couldn't remember the last time he'd danced.

Maddie's scent drifted on the night breeze. She smelled like summer, sweet and sunny. His hand on her back felt warm, comfortable, as if they had been dancing together for years. He breathed her and the night in, feeling more vulnerable than he had in weeks.

He spotted the cowboy standing at the edge of the crowd. The lights glittered and reflected off the cowboy's large silver belt buckle, which featured letters *B-O*. The infamous Bo Evans?

Maddie's warm fingers on Shane's shoulder tightened, and he could feel the pounding of her heart.

"Don't worry," Shane said, his voice sounding husky. "I won't let him bother you, if that's what you're afraid of."

She glanced up at him, her blue eyes widening a little as she met his gaze. She frowned as if she didn't know who he was talking about.

"That cowboy. The one—"

She emitted a soft chuckle. "I'm not worried about him." Her gaze seemed to soften at his confusion. Her lips curled up in a wry smile before she shook her head and looked away.

He knew she was scared. Why deny it? When her

gaze came back to his, her lips parted as if she was going to tell him the truth. His breath caught in his throat as her eyes locked with his.

Shane started when he was tapped on the shoulder. Instantly he stiffened, expecting to see Bo Evans. There was no way he was turning Maddie over to the man. No matter what she said about not being afraid of him.

"You're not trying to steal my woman, are you, cowboy?" Jud grinned as he cut in, glancing from Shane to Maddie. Shane let go of Maddie, and she stepped back as if she was as relieved as he was for the interruption.

Shane felt oddly shaken. What had happened on the dance floor? *Nothing,* he thought.

When Shane turned back, he spotted Bo Evans watching Jud and Maddie dance. Trouble. Wondering what Maddie had to fear from him gave Shane something to think about other than what he'd felt out on the dance floor just before Jud cut in.

Bo Evans watched the bitch dancing with one man then another. Both strangers.

"Who is that?" he asked, grabbing the arm of a local girl at the edge of the dance floor.

She looked startled. "Who?"

"The man dancing with Maddie Cavanaugh."

The girl smiled as if speaking of a teen idol. *"Jud Corbett."*

"Who the hell is that?" Bo asked, hating the way she had made it sound as if anyone with a brain should know that.

"He's a Hollywood stuntman. He's working in

Canada now, but he'll be shooting a movie here next month."

"Stuntman?" Bo repeated, and turned his attention back to Maddie. How was it that Maddie seemed to know this Jud Corbett? "How long's he been in town?"

The girl shrugged. "His family bought up a whole bunch of land including, my dad said, the old Trails West Ranch."

Bo scowled. He left town for a few months and everything changed. What was Maddie doing back here anyway? He'd been shocked to see her. He'd thought she'd never show her face around here again. Obviously she didn't have the good sense to stay away.

Just seeing her made him feel things he didn't want to feel. Like anger and desire.

The worst part was he didn't want to feel a damned thing for Maddie. The bitch had broken his heart, and made him look bad.

The song ended and Bo waited, hoping Jud Corbett left Maddie alone again. No such luck. The two walked toward a fancy pickup parked a few rows down from Bo's beater car.

Bo followed them as far as his car, cursing the way his life had been going. First Maddie had left, then his own mother turned against him. Not only had she refused to give him any money anymore but she'd forced him out of the house. Then she'd threatened to sell the place—his inheritance, and not give him a dime. She'd told him to get a job and earn his own money.

And now Maddie was back in town and dating a stuntman?

He was surrounded by heartless bitches, he thought, as he saw two men leaning against his car.

Bo knew at once that he either owed them money or he'd ripped them off. Since they didn't look familiar, they'd probably been sent by the person he'd ticked off. Not that it mattered. He was dead meat either way.

He started to veer off, pretending he hadn't seen them and that it wasn't his heap of a car they were leaning against.

But the bigger of the two pushed himself off the car and stepped in front of Bo, blocking his way.

The man dropped one huge paw of a hand on Bo's shoulder. "Mr. Evans?" The man had a deep voice, and the strong hand on Bo's shoulder felt capable of creating a lot of pain.

While lying came as easily as breathing, Bo sensed this was the one time in his life that the truth might be less painful. "Yes?"

"A word with you," the man said, and nodded toward his buddy.

"Sure," Bo said, sounding a hell of a lot more cheerful than he felt. He glanced around, but the parking lot was empty. Everyone who hadn't already left was still at the dance. Even the stuntman and Maddie were gone.

"Let's take a ride," the second man said. He was only a little smaller than the first guy, but he looked meaner. He wore a John Deere cap and a sullen expression.

Taking a ride with this twosome was the last thing Bo wanted to do, but the big one flashed a gun before he shoved him behind the wheel and climbed into the seat behind him.

The guy wearing the John Deere cap slid into the passenger seat. "You probably know somewhere quiet we can go to talk."

Bo contemplated his options as he tried unsuccessfully to put the key in the ignition.

"Calm down," the man next to him said with a chuckle. He took the keys from Bo and slid a key into the ignition. "Me and my friend, Dude, here, just want to talk to you. Isn't that right, Dude?"

"That's right, Earl Ray," the big man said with a chuckle.

Sure. Dude and Earl Ray? Were these guys for real?

Bo silently cursed Maddie. If all his attention hadn't been on her and the stuntman, he would have seen these two sooner and avoided what was sure as hell going to be an ugly ending to the night—if not his life.

He got the car going and drove out of town toward Bowdoin, a wildlife refuge only a few minutes out of Whitehorse. He hadn't planned to go out there. Hell, he'd just started driving out of town, not knowing where to go, too nervous to think.

But now he realized that Bowdoin was a good place to take these guys. There was at least one armed federal warden out there. With luck, the game warden would see Bo's old beater and become suspicious and come investigate.

There was a good chance of that happening since Bo and his car were known in the area for all the wrong reasons.

He drove down the narrow paved road that had been patched too many times and turned into the refuge, avoiding the headquarters building. He didn't want the two men to think he was up to anything.

When he got down the dirt road, through a stand of Russian olive trees and around a narrow turn beside an expanse of cattails, Bo felt the big hand of Dude drop onto his shoulder again.

"Pull over."

Bo pulled into a wide spot. Earl Ray reached across the seat and pulled out the keys.

"Cut your lights."

Bo did as he was told, his heart lodged in his throat. He hoped they did whatever they planned to do quickly. Would they shoot him right here in the car? And then what—walk all the way back to town?

No, they'd tell him to get out, and then they'd shoot, stab or pulverize him.

He saw the flicker of headlights in his rearview mirror and felt a surge of hope. The warden would be armed and suspicious of Bo Evans out here with these two bad-looking guys.

But the vehicle didn't approach. Instead, it slowed, its headlights going out as the driver pulled over thirty yards back up the road. Not the game warden, Bo realized with a sinking feeling. He hadn't even thought to check to see if they'd been followed. No doubt it was Dude and Earl Ray's ride home.

A trickle of sweat ran down Bo's cheek. "Can't you at least tell me what this is about?" he asked, hating that his voice sounded whiny and scared spitless.

"It's about your old girlfriend," Earl Ray said, pushing back the John Deere cap. "Excuse me, former fiancée."

Bo shot a look at the man. An almost full moon hung over the refuge, spilling a silver sheen over the landscape as well as the car.

"What?" Bo's mind raced. Why would these guys care about Maddie?

"Maddie Cavanaugh. You do remember her, right?"

Bo nodded numbly. "But what—"

"We need your help finding her."

He stared at the man. "You have to be kidding."

"Do I look like I'm kidding?" Earl Ray asked. Bo felt Dude's big paw on his shoulder again.

He winced at the pain as the big man's fingers dug into his flesh. "I thought you were joking because she was at the dance tonight."

"I thought she didn't live here anymore."

"So did I. I guess she's back."

"Where can we find her?"

"How should I know?" Bo quickly changed his tone. "I mean, it isn't like we're close, you know. I didn't even know she was back in town until tonight."

"Then you don't know where she's staying?"

"But I can find out," he added quickly. "Why would you want Maddie, though?"

Earl Ray just stared at him with that blank don't-mess-with-me look that Bo himself tried to perfect.

"The breakup wasn't friendly?" Earl Ray asked.

"The bitch broke my heart."

"Then you might be persuaded to help us?"

"What's in it for me?" Bo braced himself for more pain from the man in the back, but was surprised when both men laughed.

"You are everything we heard you were when we asked around town about you," Earl Ray said. "A man after my own heart. Did I mention we are willing to compensate you?"

Compensation. Music to Bo's ears. "Let's talk money, then," Bo said, relaxing now.

Chapter Five

"What did you say to her?" Jud demanded the next morning.

"What?" Shane looked up as his youngest brother sat down at the breakfast table. His mind had been a thousand miles away. In Texas.

"Maddie. What did you say to her?"

"Oh, her," Shane said, and went back to his breakfast.

"What do you mean, 'Oh, her'?" Jud demanded.

Shane looked up at him again, wondering who'd put a burr under his saddle this morning. "Look, I didn't say anything to her. I just picked her up and took her to the rodeo grounds like you asked me to."

"So you didn't talk to her?"

Shane put down his fork. "What is your problem?"

"I got the impression that you were rude to her. She was upset after dancing with you."

Shane recalled the dance. The memory hadn't gotten far away. "I wasn't the one who upset her. It was some cowboy. Bo Evans. I suspect he's an old boyfriend."

He didn't add that the cowboy had followed Jud and Maddie to the parking lot when they'd left the rodeo dance last night. Shane had feared there might be trouble, so he'd tailed Bo. And there might have been— if there hadn't been two thugs waiting for the cowboy by his car. The three had left together, but the meeting hadn't looked cordial.

"Maddie's a nice girl."

"Yeah," Shane said, locking eyes with his brother.

"You got something to say?" Jud challenged.

Shane picked up his fork and returned to his breakfast, even though he wasn't hungry anymore. The memory of the dance, the feel of her in his arms, had put him off his feed. Something about the woman had gotten to him. He didn't want to see her hurt.

And Maddie Cavanaugh was headed for trouble. If not from her old boyfriend, Bo, then from Jud. And Shane would hate to see that happen.

But, he reminded himself, Maddie was none of his business.

"I have to return to the set today," Jud said. "But I'll be back as soon as I can."

Shane said nothing, but he hoped his brother would get tired of this long-distance romance with Maddie. The woman deserved better. And if Shane was right about Bo, Maddie already had her share of heartbreak from falling for the wrong man.

MADDIE CAVANAUGH woke to the smell of pancakes. She rolled over, smiling to herself at the thought of her cousin's breakfasts. That was one of the joys of coming home.

Home. She did feel at home here. She'd made so many excuses not to come back to Old Town White-horse. Her childhood home was sold and gone, not that she ever wanted to return to it. Nothing but bad memories there.

She'd missed her cousins and hadn't realized how much she'd missed the land. Just being able to ride her horse across the open country and down to the Missouri Breaks gave her a sense of freedom and hope.

It was good to be back at a place she knew so well.

At the sound of murmured voices, Maddie got up and dressed. Her great-aunt had seen to it that her room was furnished with some of her own things. Maddie hadn't given a thought to any of her possessions when she'd left. None of it had mattered.

But now she was thankful that her favorite things from childhood had been saved. Tears welled in her eyes as she picked up a cherish doll from a shelf in the closet. Behind it, in a clear plastic bag, was her handmade baby quilt that, as far as she knew, had never been used.

Maddie started to reach for the quilt, then pulled her hand back at the thought of her mother. She didn't know why the quilt would remind her of her mother. Sarah Cavanaugh had never belonged to the Whitehorse Sewing Circle. As far as she knew, her mother had never sewn anything in her life, let alone helped make her birth quilt.

Sarah was more about putting on a good face. That was why she bought such expensive things for their home, things Maddie's father, Roy, couldn't afford. The baby quilt she'd bagged up and put in the attic. Maddie always thought her mother would have thrown it away if she hadn't feared the Whitehorse Sewing Circle women would find out and thinking her ungrateful for not appreciating the gift for her baby daughter.

Maddie hadn't realized the strain on her parents' marriage or how obsessed her mother was about being a pillar of Old Town Whitehorse society. It all seemed ludicrous to Maddie, but her mother would have done anything to feel that people looked up to her.

That part of Maddie's life was still painful. She could never forgive her mother for what she'd done, and that made her both sad and filled with guilt. How could she not love her own mother?

Pushing those thoughts as far away as possible, Maddie headed for the kitchen. As she wandered into the bright, warm room, she felt the weight of the past lift from her shoulders. These people were her family.

Her cousin Laci was busy making pancakes, looking funny in the apron that billowed out from her very pregnant belly. She had a spatula in her hand and a big smile on her face.

Aunt Pearl was at the table, her cane leaning against her chair. She'd recovered well from her stroke but still had trouble getting around.

Maddie went to place a kiss on her great-aunt's cheek.

"Laney's on her way over," Laci said of her sister. Laney and her husband, Nick, a deputy sheriff, lived in the house they'd built up the road. "There's chokecherry syrup, real butter, bacon and ham to go with the pancakes."

"Of course," Maddie said with a laugh, as she joined her great-aunt at the table. Laci, who had always cooked huge meals, shared her love of cooking with her husband. The two now owned the Northern Lights restaurant and lived in the apartment over it. But Laci spent a lot of time here taking care of her grandparents.

Maddie breathed in the familiar scents and told herself that coming back hadn't been a mistake. She even liked the waitressing job at Northern Lights. Laci had offered to teach her to cook, but Maddie preferred to serve food until she decided what she wanted to do with her life.

"Who was that I saw you dancing with last night?" Laci asked, giving Maddie a playful nudge as she slipped a plate of pancakes in front of her.

"Jud Corbett. He's the stuntman you and Laney talked me into going out with."

"Not him. The tall, dark and seriously awesome one."

Definitely serious, Maddie thought. She swallowed and checked her expression before looking up. "That was Jud's brother, Shane." She could feel her great-aunt's gaze on her. Her cheeks heated at the memory of being in Shane's arms on the dance floor. There had been that moment, right before Jud had cut in…

"Shane saved me from Bo," Maddie blurted out, as if she needed an excuse for dancing with Shane.

"Bo's back?" Aunt Pearl asked in her stilted post-stroke cadence.

"I'm afraid so, but it's fine." In fact, she was surprised Bo hadn't been her first thought this morning.

For so long, he had been. She'd been shaken and upset at just the sight of him, but after dancing with Shane and then Jud, she'd actually forgotten about Bo. She had thought he'd left town. Obviously he was back, as well.

"I can handle Bo," she said, seeing Laci's concern and wishing she hadn't brought him up.

"Of course you can," Aunt Pearl said.

"Good morning, everyone!" Laney called. She entered the kitchen, looking just as pregnant as her sister. "Did you have fun last night?" she asked Maddie, as she passed her chair. Apparently everyone in town had seen her dancing with the Corbett brothers.

"She saw Bo," Laci said.

Laney stopped in midstep and turned to look back at Maddie, worry furrowing her brow.

"It was fine," Maddie assured her. "Shane Corbett cut him off and danced with me until Jud arrived. I didn't see Bo after that. Really, I haven't given him a thought."

"So you didn't talk to Bo?" Laney asked.

"There is nothing to say. Bo is history." That at least was true. Bo was part of her bad memories. "I can't believe you two are due at almost the same time," Maddie said, changing the subject. "I won't be surprised if you have your babies on the same day. Do you have names picked out yet?"

She cut her pancakes and took a bite as she listened to her cousins laughing and joking.

"We both want to name our babies Jack," Laci was saying. "So the first one who delivers gets the name."

Maddie laughed, feeling blessed. She was home with

her family. She tried not to think about what a disappointment her parents had been. That was the past. And the future? A certain Corbett came to mind at the thought.

LATER THAT MORNING, as Maddie headed for work, she took the long way so she wouldn't have to drive by her old house or Geraldine Shaw's place. Geraldine had been the mother she'd never had, and Maddie mourned her death.

She hadn't gone far when she glanced in her rearview mirror and saw a rusted red car coming up fast behind her.

She'd known even before she caught a glimpse of Bo's face behind the wheel that it would be him. He leaned on the horn, startling her.

The gravel road was narrow. She'd have to pull over or almost drive into the ditch to let him pass. She had no intention of doing either.

He laid on the horn again. When she glanced in her rearview mirror, she saw that he'd rolled down his window and was motioning for her to pull over.

There was a time when she would have been afraid not to do as Bo demanded.

But that time had long since passed. She sped up, willing herself not to look in the mirror, not to react to his incessant honking.

He stayed right with her all five miles to town, riding her back bumper the whole way. She could almost feel his anger and frustration. Bo wouldn't forget this. The next time she ran into him—

She shuddered and shoved the thought away. At the edge of town, she headed for Main Street, wondering how far Bo would go.

As she slowed, she saw that he was still right behind her. She pulled into the sheriff's department parking lot, remembering another time she'd come here looking for help. Bo had stopped her that time.

She cut the engine and got out, not looking in his direction even when she heard his car come to a screeching stop in the middle of the street.

"Maddie! Hey, I'm talking to you!"

She couldn't possibly miss the fury and frustration in his voice as she started toward the sheriff's office. Nor could she pretend Bo wasn't scaring her.

"I want to talk to you, bitch!" he yelled, as she reached the entrance. His engine revved as she pulled open the outer door and stepped into the tiny alcove. Out of the corner of her eye, she saw his car take off, tires smoking, engine clanking.

Maddie leaned against the closed door, fighting tears. She knew that if she reported the incident to the sheriff, he'd talk to Bo and warn him to leave her alone.

That would just make things worse. She knew Bo Evans. Her coming here had made him angry enough. She couldn't depend on anyone to protect her from him. He would get to her. It was just a matter of time.

Maddie knew she'd eventually have to face him. It was the only way to put an end to his harassment.

But as she waited just inside the outer door, she told herself she had an advantage.

Unlike Bo, Maddie had changed. She wasn't the

woman who had let Bo mistreat her. That woman was gone. But Bo Evans didn't know that. Not yet, anyway.

SHANE COULDN'T BELIEVE what he was doing. He'd sworn he wouldn't get involved in his brother's love life.

In fact, when Jud called this morning, Shane had told him no.

"I just need you to drop something off at the restaurant," Jud had said.

"Sorry."

"I wouldn't ask, but it's Maddie's wallet. It must have fallen out of her purse last night. I doubt she's even realized I have it, but she will the moment she needs to buy gas. I left the wallet on the table by the front door. I'm really sorry to have to ask you to do this."

Shane had sworn under his breath. "Maybe Dad can do it."

"He's already left," Jud said. "Neither Juanita or Kate are going into town today. They're doing some canning, so they're tied up. I know it's a lot to ask…"

That was just it. Dropping off the wallet wasn't a lot to ask, and Jud knew it.

"This is the last time," Shane said.

"I doubt you'll ever have to return her wallet again," Jud said. "Thanks for doing this, Shane. I won't forget it."

He'd felt like a heel, making such a big deal out of dropping off a wallet.

But as he drove into Whitehorse, he still wanted to kick himself from here to Sunday for agreeing to do it. He had a feeling he was the last person Maddie wanted to see after the way he'd acted at the rodeo.

He told himself that with any luck it would take no more than a few minutes, and she wouldn't even have to see him. He'd just drop off the wallet and hightail it back to the ranch.

But as he turned down the street, he saw Maddie pull up in front of the sheriff's office and Bo Evan's battered red car pull up in the middle of the street right behind her.

Shane pulled over a few parking spots down, got out and walked down the street toward them. He couldn't hear what the cowboy yelled at Maddie as she exited her truck, but Shane was glad she had the sense to enter the sheriff's office rather than confront the man.

Shane got a good a view of Bo's furious face right before the cowboy gunned the engine and took off.

What bothered Shane was that Bo didn't go far. He pulled over down the block.

The last thing Shane wanted to do was get involved. Hell, he wanted nothing to do with any of this. But whether or not Jud was serious about Maddie, Shane couldn't just sit back and let something bad happen to her.

Cursing under his breath, he walked down the street to where Bo was sitting in his beat-up car. The cowboy had his gaze on his rearview mirror, obviously waiting for Maddie to leave the sheriff's office.

Shane had run across men like this one too many times during his law-enforcement career.

All of Bo's attention was on the front door of the sheriff's department, so the bastard didn't even notice him until Shane jerked open the car door and dragged Bo out.

"Hey! What the—"

Shane slammed him against the side of the car. "I don't know what your story is or who the hell you are, and I don't care. Leave Maddie Cavanaugh alone."

"I'm Bo Evans, her…fiancé, you dumb bastard."

"You're not her fiancé anymore."

The cowboy puffed up even more, plainly yearning for a fight. "Yeah? Says who?"

"Says the young woman. It's clear she wants nothing to do with you. Now leave her alone. I'm asking you nicely. I won't be so nice next time."

"I recognize you," Bo said, squinting at Shane. "You danced with Maddie at the rodeo. You a cop or somethin'?"

"Or something." Shane started to turn his back on Bo, knowing that only then would the cowboy make his move. Men like Bo Evans were so predictable.

Sure enough Bo came at him with a roundhouse swing. Shane blocked it and caught him in the midsection with an elbow. Bo doubled over, falling back against his car.

"Don't let me catch you near Maddie again." Shane turned and walked back down the street. That had been a fool's errand. Men like Bo Evans didn't take no for an answer. While Shane meant what he said, he doubted Bo was going to take the threat seriously.

Shane then saw Maddie approach the Northern Lights restaurant. There hadn't been time for her to report Bo to the sheriff. Shane guessed that going into the sheriff's office had been just a ruse on her part. She'd never intended to report her former fiancé.

He hoped to hell Maddie knew what she was doing. Bo Evans was dangerous. But he suspected she already knew that.

Just before she ducked into the restaurant, Shane saw her look up the street to where Bo was still parked. Then her glance shifted to Shane. She frowned as if she knew what he'd been up to—and wasn't happy about him butting into her business.

BO EVANS FOUGHT to catch his breath as he watched the man walk away. For a moment, he thought about going after the cocky bastard or maybe pressing assault charges.

Yeah. Like the sheriff would believe anything he told him. No, Bo knew if there was going to be any justice he'd have to get it himself. And he would.

Just as he would get his hands on Maddie.

A deadly mixture of frustration, anger and pain swelled inside him to the point where he thought he might explode. Turning, he proceeded to kick the rusting metal panels of his car until his feet hurt more than his pride, then slam his fist down onto the already dented roof until his knuckles bled.

His rage having run its course, Bo fell against the side of his car.

All he had wanted to do was talk to Maddie.

At least that's what he'd convinced himself he'd planned to do. Not harm her. Hell, maybe he was planning to warn her about the men who were after her.

But that was before the bitch had gone to the sheriff. Now all bets were off. Maddie deserved whatever happened to her. He could have saved her. He liked that her safety had been in his hands. Still was.

But now he was going to feed her to the dogs.

Bo wiped the blood from his hands on his jeans and considered what to do next. He was glad he'd told Earl Ray and Dude that he'd bring them Maddie. They were waiting at a motel down by the Milk River. They'd offered him money, which he damned well intended to collect.

Maddie Cavanaugh would rue the day she crossed Bo Evans, he thought as he plotted how he was going to get to her.

As Maddie let the door close behind her, she called hello to Laci's husband, Bridger, who was busy cooking in the back of the restaurant and went to change into her uniform for her lunch shift.

She refused to think about Bo. He wasn't going to spoil this for her. She was home and she was staying.

And as for Shane Corbett…

As if she'd conjured him up, Shane pushed open the door to the restaurant, making her realize that she'd forgotten to lock it behind her.

"We don't open for another twenty minutes," she said, trying to sound calmer than she felt. She was angry with herself for leaving the door open. Angrier still that she'd let Bo upset her to the point that she'd forgotten.

And then there was Shane.

What brought him by this time? she wondered.

"I didn't come by for lunch," Shane said, looking ill at ease. He wore jeans, boots and a red-and-blue checked shirt that brought out the blue in his eyes.

Maggie hated that the man unnerved her as much as she hated that every time she turned around he was there rescuing her.

"I just stopped by to drop off your wallet," Shane said, digging into his pocket. "I guess you dropped it in Jud's rig. He asked me to bring it by, thought you'd need it."

Maddie felt her cheeks burn with irritation. She'd dropped her wallet and Jud sent his big brother to return it? "Thank you," she managed to say, and stepped forward to take it from him.

"No problem."

"If that's all, I need to get my tables set up before the lunch crowd arrives," she said.

"Sure," he said backing toward the door as if anxious to escape.

Fortunately the door closed behind him before he heard her swear, something she seldom did. Didn't the man see what was going on? Apparently not.

Maddie knew she shouldn't be irritated with Shane. This was all Jud's doing. She couldn't wait to see Jud and give him a piece of her mind.

The lunch shift passed quickly, the restaurant so busy it kept her mind off Bo. And Shane. And Jud.

Maddie was surprised how many of the patrons she didn't know. The town had grown since she'd left.

When her shift was over, she changed from her uniform back into jeans, boots and a Western shirt, hesitating before she left to glance out the front restaurant windows.

A few large white cumulous clouds floated in the

blue sky. Maddie loved summer days and couldn't wait to get back out to the Cavanaugh's ranch so she could ride her horse before her next shift. Her cousins had been boarding it there for her since she left town.

She didn't see Bo's car, but she knew that didn't mean anything. If she knew Bo, which she did, his next attack would be without warning.

As she passed a preset table for the dinner meal, Maddie slipped one of the steak knives into her purse.

Chapter Six

For the rest of the afternoon, all Shane wanted was to sit in the shade on the porch and read a book he'd picked up on Montana.

But the window to the living room was open, and he couldn't help but overhear the conversation between Kate and his father.

"I think I'll just stay around here," Kate said. "I have some things I want to do. You don't mind, do you?"

"Of course not," Grayson said. "I just worry about you staying out here on the ranch all the time."

"I love it here. There is really no other place I want to be."

Shane heard his father's voice soften even more and knew he was holding his new bride.

"I'll see you later then," Grayson said. "Don't overdo it. I worry about you sometimes."

Grayson was no fool. He must have noticed that Kate had been unusually quiet when she returned from town the other day. Shane remembered his father commenting on how pale she appeared and asking if she was feeling ill.

"I'm fine," Kate had said. "I think it was the heat. It's so much hotter in town than out here."

Now Grayson came out the front door, hesitating when he spotted his son. Shane watched him look back into the house, then come over to the porch rocker.

"Russell and I are driving up to Loring," Grayson said. "Interested in coming along?"

Shane shook his head. "Thanks, but I really want to finish this book." He hoped his father didn't push it. To his relief, Grayson didn't.

His father studied the cover of the Montana history book and then him. "Kate's running a little tired. She's staying home. Would you mind, since you're going to be here, just keeping an eye on her?"

Shane groaned inwardly. The last thing he needed was his father asking him to keep an eye on Kate. He'd already been doing that behind both of their backs.

"Sure. No problem," he said.

His father laid a hand on his shoulder. "Thanks. I didn't realize how hard it would be on her, coming back here, you know?"

Shane nodded, although he didn't know. What was it about coming back here that was so hard? Obviously Grayson believed it was because Kate's father had died here and the family had lost the ranch.

Shane suspected there was more to it and was even more convinced when not thirty minutes after Grayson had left, Kate came out carrying her purse and car keys.

"I need to run into town," Kate said. "Need to pick up something I forgot."

"Would you like me to go for you?" Shane asked putting down his book, trying hard not to let her see that he was on to her.

"No, but thank you," she said, as she hurried down the steps. "I won't be long."

"Drive carefully," he called after her.

Shane gave her over a few minutes start before he headed for his pickup.

CHESTER BAILEY LOOKED UP as he came out of the Hi-Line Café, his footsteps faltering when he saw Kate.

"Running into each other two times in the same amount of days must be a record," Chester said, clearly flustered.

"This time it wasn't accidental," Kate said. "I need to talk to you."

Chester glanced back at the café, as if he were afraid Susie would see them together. "Sure. About what?"

Kate took a breath and let it out slowly. "Is there somewhere we could go?"

He looked at her as if she'd just suggested they get a motel.

"A place we could talk in private. How about the park?"

"The park?" Chester repeated.

"Trafton Park." Kate felt her patience slipping. The park was on the Milk River, just a few blocks away. "I'll meet you there."

He nodded, but she wondered if he would show up, given the way he was acting.

Kate got back in her SUV and drove to the park. She pulled under the shade of one of the large old cottonwoods and got out to sit at a picnic table. The day was pure Montana June—only a few clouds in the crystalline blue sky, the temperature just warm enough to be pleasant.

She fidgeted, trying to talk herself out of what she was about to do when Chester pulled up in his truck. He couldn't have looked more awkward as he climbed out and joined her, taking a seat on the opposite side of the picnic table.

"What's this about, Kate?" he asked, his voice wavering a little.

She stared at him, wondering what she'd seen in him all those years ago. She hadn't been that young or that naïve. But she had been hurting, and for a while Chester had made her feel better.

Now she knew it hadn't been honor or loyalty that had motivated him to make the decision he had. It had been cowardice. Chester Bailey was a man who always took the easy way out.

Or was that just her anger toward the man who'd hurt her?

"What do you think this is about?" she snapped, unable to contain that anger any longer. She knew she wasn't being fair, since most of that anger was directed at herself.

He looked as if she'd slapped him.

"I'm sorry, but I've been struggling with the past," she said, unable to keep the sarcasm out of her tone.

He sighed. "Kate, all that was so long ago, who can even remember—"

"*I* remember." She'd told herself she wasn't going to do this. "I remember being pregnant and scared and completely alone."

"You know why I couldn't—"

"Yes." She reminded herself that she hadn't asked him here to dredge up the past hurt—at least not between them. "I need to tell you something." This was going to be harder than she thought. "I didn't lose the baby."

He stared at her. *"What?"*

"I didn't lose the baby." All those years ago she'd sent him a note telling him she'd miscarried. She hadn't wanted him to know the truth because he'd made it clear he didn't care. "I gave the baby up for adoption."

He shook his head, his look one of shock. "You lied to me?"

"It was a baby girl. That's all I know except that she was adopted by someone from around here."

"I don't believe you."

"It's true. I left right away but you might've even gotten to watch her grow up. Your own daughter, right here in Whitehorse."

"I can't do this, Kate." He started for his truck, running away as he always had.

"I'm going to find her." Her words surprised her. She'd stayed away all these years, keeping busy with a newspaper career, not looking back. But then she'd found that damned box of photographs of her and Rebecca from their time on the Trails West Ranch, and since she was going to be in Austin anyway, she'd taken them by Grayson Corbett's ranch.

Chester turned back toward her, the desperation in his face making him look older than he was. "After all these years of believing our baby died and now… How could you have done that to me? Did you hate me that much?"

"Yes," she said honestly.

He stared at her, the raw pain in his face filling her with guilt. Then he turned and left without looking back.

Kate covered her face with her hands as she listened to the crunch of the pickup's tires on the gravel.

SHANE WATCHED Kate from a distance. He hated this, but protecting his father was second nature. Grayson had clearly been under Kate's spell from the beginning. Buying the Trails West Ranch and moving to Montana had been impulsive—and wasn't like his father. Grayson had always been so careful in his business dealings, amassing a fortune.

That was another thing that worried Shane about Kate. She had shown up on Grayson's doorstep out of the blue with the excuse that she'd found a box of old photographs of Rebecca.

It had happened too fast. The courtship, the marriage and this move. On top of that, since coming to Montana Kate had been acting oddly.

Shane had noticed how hesitant she seemed about going into town. Now he thought he knew why as he watched the man leave. Then, the other day she'd run into that older man outside the store. Shane had seen how nervous and awkward she'd been. It was clear Kate and the man knew each other.

Now Shane knew it was time to find out who this man from Kate's past was—and, if possible, what he'd meant to her.

He followed the man back to a café on the edge of the town. Getting out, he went into the Hi-Line café, ordered a cup of coffee and struck up a conversation with the waitress, a young high-school student.

He'd found out that the man's name was Chester Bailey. Bailey's daughter, Eve, was married to Sheriff Carter Jackson and lived on the home ranch south of Old Town Whitehorse. Another daughter, McKenna, raised paint horses with her husband on a separate place to the west of the old Bailey place. A third daughter, Faith Bailey, lived in Bozeman.

Chester and Lila, who had been married for thirty years, were divorced. Lila had remarried and was now living in Florida.

Chester and the other owner of the café, Susie, were an item. Chester was a former rancher—a little shy but sweet, according to the waitress who apparently knew everyone in town.

Angry with himself butting into his stepmother's business, Shane finished his coffee and left. He drove around for a while then, as if his pickup had a mind of its own, he drove down Main Street past the Northern Lights restaurant and saw Maddie's pickup parked across the street.

He checked his watch. The restaurant should just now be reopening for the evening. His stomach growled, and while common sense told him to keep on going, he turned in and parked.

After all, he had to eat. He wasn't going to be able to pass the physical to return to the Texas Rangers unless he took better care of himself.

The truth was he couldn't get Maddie off his mind. He told himself he had to warn her about Bo Evans. And while he was at it, maybe warn her about Jud. Then he could wash his hands of the whole mess with a clear conscience.

Maddie looked up as Shane entered the restaurant. Surprise registered in her gaze and was followed instantly by irritation.

"I'll be right with you. Sit wherever you'd like," she called to him, as she disappeared into the kitchen.

The place was empty. He chose a table in the corner so he could face the door, an old habit.

Maddie smiled politely as she returned with a menu, a glass of iced water and a small basket of warm, thickly sliced bread.

His stomach growled at the smell of the bread. Her smile broadened as she heard it.

"The special this evening is tomato-cheese ravioli with Italian salad," she said.

He handed her back the unopened menu as his stomach rumbled again. "The special it is." He smiled, embarrassed more by his own nervousness than his hungry stomach. This woman unnerved him.

"You won't be sorry," she said, as she took the menu. "Enjoy the bread. In the basket, there's honey butter in a small crock. Your supper will be right up."

As she turned and walked away, Shane told himself that she made him edgy because of her relationship with his brother—or lack of one. Jud had hardly seen Maddie. He bet his little brother had a woman or two on the set. He always did.

The bread with the honey butter was nothing short of amazing. He had the place to himself and almost hoped more diners would come in so he wouldn't be tempted to try to talk to Maddie about Bo and Jud.

Maddie brought out his meal, the ravioli smelling heavenly. For a guy born and raised on Tex-Mex, he was surprised by how much he enjoyed his Italian supper.

He'd finished every bite and eaten his salad and all the bread when Maddie came back to see if he wanted dessert.

"We have a flourless chocolate torte that my cousin makes," she said. "It's worth every calorie."

"I'll take it and some coffee if you'll sit with me for a few minutes," he said.

She hesitated, clearly uncertain even though she wasn't busy. "All right," she said after a moment. She left, returning with the torte and two cups of coffee.

As she took the chair across from him, he noted that the freckles on her face seemed to stand out more than they had earlier. Her eyes were a bright, clear blue. And when she peered at him over the rim of her coffee cup, her gaze seemed almost challenging.

"I want to talk to you about Jud," he said, and could have kicked himself.

She slowly put down the cup, her eyebrow lifting as she cocked her head at him.

"The thing about Jud is that he's young and impulsive," Shane said.

Still Maddie said nothing, that blue gaze of hers never wavering. She seemed to be waiting for him to dig himself in deeper.

"He has a tendency to sweep a woman off her feet, especially when he's doing his Hollywood stuntman thing." Shane wished she would say something, but when she still didn't, he stumbled on: "What I'm trying to say is that I just don't want to see you get hurt."

"You're worried about your brother hurting me?" Maddie asked, sounding almost amused.

"You wouldn't be the first woman he's led on," Shane said, suddenly feeling horribly disloyal. "But this time it's different because you aren't even his type."

"I see. So you're saying there isn't any way Jud could be serious about someone like me?"

"No—" Shane rubbed the back of his neck "—it's more complicated than that."

She crossed her arms over her chest, clearly waiting for him to continue.

He sighed. Maddie deserved the truth, didn't she? He just didn't want to be the one to tell her. If he thought for an instant that Jud might be serious about her he wouldn't have started this to begin with.

"Look, I'm going to be straight with you," he said. "My mother died right after Jud and Dalton were born. I barely remember her, but my father was heartbroken. Until he met Kate Wade, he'd always said there was no other woman for him."

Maddie had an "And your point is?" look on her face.

He rushed on. "All these years, my father couldn't bring himself to go through my mother's things. Until—"

"Kate?" Maddie offered.

"Yeah. So when he finally did go through her things he found some letters. One for each of her sons to be read on our wedding days. My mother also left a letter for my father. Apparently she feared he would raise us to be like him, wild and untethered. She was afraid that since we wouldn't have a mother, we wouldn't appreciate the need for a woman in our lives until it was too late."

Maddie's eyes widened. "You have to be kidding."

"Afraid not. She wanted my father to do everything in his power to see that we were each married before the age of thirty-five. Right now my oldest brother is thirty-two and unmarried. Her dying wish was that we would each marry a Montana cowgirl, just like she had been when she met my father." He rushed on before he lost his courage. "So we drew straws to see who would get married first."

"Jud drew the shortest straw."

Shane nodded, waiting for his words to sink in. So far Maddie's reaction had been one of almost amusement.

"What straw did you draw?"

He stared at her for a moment, surprised by the unexpected question. "The longest one, but I think the whole thing is ludicrous and I have no intention of going along with it."

"You think Jud is, though."

"The thing is, even if it wasn't our mother's dying wish, Jud doesn't want to hurt our father. Since he moved up here, Dad seems determined to get us all to settle here, preferably on the Trails West Ranch."

"I see." She picked up her coffee cup and took a sip before putting it down again.

He'd expected her to be heartbroken or at least angry. "I just felt you should know what's going on."

She smiled at that. "I had a pretty good idea what was going on, but you've definitely helped me see it more clearly." She looked up, meeting his gaze. "Anything else you'd like to share with me?"

Shane swallowed. Warning her about Jud hadn't worked. He might as well give the other matter a shot.

"I saw Bo Evans harassing you the other day," he said.

Her expression didn't change.

"I wouldn't say anything but I'm worried about you."

Another cock of her eyebrow and that amused look. "You are?"

"The man is dangerous. But I suspect you already know that. I think you need to get a restraining order against him."

She smiled as she ran her finger along the rim of her coffee cup. "You really think that would deter Bo?"

"No, but it would let him know you mean business and make the sheriff aware of the problem."

Maddie chuckled as she looked at him. He found himself hypnotized by the tiny gold flecks floating in all that blue. "I'm touched by your concern. Really," Maddie said, although her tone suggested otherwise.

"I was a Texas Ranger." *Was.* He started to correct himself but continued. "I guess butting into other people's business is in my blood."

Maddie smiled at that. "So you're just telling me

these things as a lawman. I see." She rose and started to clear the table.

He touched her hand to stop her, feeling he'd made a mess of this and wanting to fix it, needing to fix it, but not having a clue how.

He felt her tremble at his touch.

"I'm not Bo Evans," he said, thinking that explained her reaction.

"I never thought you were. But the truth is, you don't know anything about me, and while I appreciate your warnings, I can take care of myself."

He feared she was wrong on both counts. He did know a lot about her and sensed even more. And he wasn't all that sure that anyone could take care of themselves when it came to Bo Evans.

Shane knew his butting in had a lot to do with the rodeo dance and that intimate moment when he'd felt a primitive connection between them.

It had scared him. Maybe scared her, too. But she was still his brother's girlfriend, and he was out of line.

"You're right, it's none of my business."

He watched her bite down on her lower lip. As she studied him, her blue eyes sparked with something he took for anger. When she opened her mouth, he'd expected her to light into him again.

"Did you like the torte?" she asked, as she brushed a lock of blond hair back from her freckled face.

Shane looked down at his plate, surprised to find the torte gone. He didn't remember eating it but could still taste the rich dark chocolate on his tongue. "It was just as wonderful as you said it was."

She smiled almost ruefully before she left him alone at the table feeling like a fool. "I'll get your check."

MADDIE LET OUT an oath the minute she was out of Shane's sight. Something she'd been doing too often lately.

"Problems?" Bridger Duvall asked as she came into the kitchen.

"If I told you, you wouldn't believe me," she said, remembering the way Jud Corbett had chased her, determined to get a date with her. It was all starting to make sense. "Why are men so…so…"

"Clueless?" Bridger asked with a grin.

Maddie smiled. "When it comes to women? Yes."

"I'd love to argue the point, but I remember how I fought admitting that I'd fallen in love with Laci. Can you imagine? The truth was she stole my heart the first time I tasted something she'd cooked. It was love at first bite."

Maddie laughed. "The two of you are made for each other. At least you realized that."

"It took me a while," he admitted. "She knew before I did."

Men, Maddie thought, as she shook her head and dug out Shane's bill. And he thought he knew his brother so well. She laughed at the thought.

"So this problem you're having with a man, I assume it's Jud Corbett?" Bridger asked.

"The moment I laid eyes on Jud, I knew exactly what to expect," she said truthfully. It was one of the reasons she hadn't wanted to go out with him. But she knew Laci and Laney were worried about how she hadn't dated since Bo.

"Time to get back on that horse that bucked you off," Laci had said, then handed her a cookie.

Maddie had laughed, and warmed by the cookie, agreed to go out with Jud, knowing she could never fall for the man.

Now she knew that he only asked her out because he'd drawn the shortest straw in some stupid marriage pact and had come up with a way out. At least now she knew what he was up to.

"Give the man a little time," Bridger suggested. "He'll come around."

Maddie pushed open the kitchen door to glance out at Shane. "We can only hope," she said under her breath, as she went out to give him his check.

She was suddenly furious with both Corbett brothers.

"What is wrong with you Corbetts?" she demanded when she reached the table.

"Where would you like me to start? It could take a while."

"You Corbett brothers wouldn't know what to do with a Montana cowgirl if you had one," she snapped.

Shane wisely said nothing.

She took a deep breath and let it out. "I hope you enjoyed your supper," she said slapping the bill down on his table. "Have a nice day."

With that she turned and stormed back toward the kitchen, feeling her face heat with embarrassment. On the way, she kicked the leg of one of the chairs, wishing it was Shane Corbett's shin.

FROM ACROSS THE STREET, Bo Evans cursed Maddie to hell and gone as he watched her with the Texas Ranger.

He'd known Shane Corbett was the law before he'd asked around and found out his name—and profession. The man carried himself with the same superiority that Bo had hated in every lawman he'd ever met. But he'd been surprised to find out that Corbett was a Texas Ranger on medical leave after being shot during an arrest.

Bo would have loved to shake the hand of the man who'd shot Shane. Unfortunately that man was dead, and Shane was alive and in Whitehorse and apparently interested in Maddie.

"Big mistake," Bo said under his breath, as he watched Shane come out of the restaurant. "Big mistake."

Bo waited until Shane drove away before he got out of his car and started across the street. He thought about going into the restaurant, backing Maddie up against the wall... He could feel his hands on her soft curves. Oh, what he wanted to do to that bitch.

But reason won out for a change, and he entered the hardware store a few doors down. He had to bide his time, think things out. Plan.

"Can I help you?" the girl behind the counter asked.

"Duct tape."

She pointed him down an aisle, where he found both duct tape and some rope used for clotheslines. A glint of metal caught his eye as he started toward the cash register. He back-stepped, smiling as he picked up a dangerous-looking pair of hedge trimmers.

"What you couldn't do with these," he said to

himself, as he snapped the blades open and closed, and thought about what he was going to do to Maddie once it got dark.

Chapter Seven

Jerilyn woke in the afternoon, hung over and confused. It took her a moment to recall where she was. At first she thought she was still with Earl Ray and sat up in bed with a start. Then she remembered she was with the man she'd picked up at the bar last night.

She could hear Buck Jones in the kitchen and smell the scent of coffee. Lying back down, she snuggled under the covers. The bedroom had a slight chill to it that reminded her she'd made it to Montana. The wallpaper in the room was covered in faded tiny yellow flowers. There was an old bureau and an antique mirror.

That was the extent of a woman's touch in the room. Jerilyn suspected the house had belonged to Buck's mother and that he hadn't changed a thing since her death.

The moment she'd seen Buck's pickup she knew he wasn't going to be much help financially. When she'd checked the contents of his wallet in the middle of the night, she'd found twenty-three dollars and some coupons for groceries. Not a good sign. Even the house was small, and from what she'd seen of Whitehorse it wouldn't bring much.

But Buck had been kind and more than a little helpful.

"Maddie Cavanaugh? Sure, I know her. Well, know *of* her," he'd said after they'd left the bar and come to his house. "She's been away at college until just recently."

"Her parents nice?"

He'd hesitated, and she'd felt her stomach roil. "Sarah's always been a little uppity, you know. Roy's nice enough. Quiet. Like a lot of ranchers."

Uppity was good.

"They have a pretty big ranch?"

"Good-sized. Brought enough when Roy sold it that he was able to relocate to Arizona, I heard."

"They don't still live here?" she asked, sounding as if she might cry.

"Divorced. Been a few years now." He shook his head. "Why the interest in the Cavanaughs?"

Jerilyn had licked her lips and decided on the truth. It was going to come out anyway. "Maddie is my natural-born child."

Buck had stared at her as if she'd grown horns. "Are you saying…"

She'd nodded. "I was sixteen," she'd said, and poured out her story, crying a little as she'd told it.

"I'm so sorry. Maddie was adopted, huh?" He shook his head. "And you've never met her?"

"My mother told me she went to a good family. I didn't want to interfere. I wasn't even supposed to know what happened to her. I guess I was afraid, too, that she might not like me."

Now as the smell of coffee grew stronger, Jerilyn sat up in bed, and Buck brought her a cup along with a stale muffin. She thanked him and sipped the hot, strong coffee and nibbled at the muffin. She was hungry.

Buck's brown eyes softened as he gazed at her. "I've been thinkin'. I bet Maddie would want to meet you."

"I don't know," Jerilyn said. "You didn't say what happened to her adoptive mother."

"Don't know. There was talk, but then there's always talk in Whitehorse. I know a lot of people were glad to see her get her comeuppance."

This didn't sound good.

"I heard she'd been involved in some blackmail scheme, but no charges were ever filed. After the divorce Sarah just up and left town, but definitely with her tail tucked between her legs, if you know what I mean."

Jerilyn knew only too well. So there was no money. Unless Maddie… "You said my daughter is back from college?"

"Yep. She's waitressing down at the Northern Lights restaurant."

A *waitress?* "There's no other family?"

"There's her cousins, Laci and Laney, and her Great Aunt Pearl and Uncle Titus."

"They're well off financially? I mean, I wouldn't want to think that my baby girl wasn't well taken care of," she added quickly.

Buck patted her hand. "No one around here's rich by any standards. Some's got a lot of land. Most just scrape by. Maddie's cousin Laney's married to a deputy. Her cousin Laci and her husband just started the restaurant. Both women are pregnant, big as houses."

"And the great aunt and uncle?"

"Pearl's doing better after her stroke. Titus, well, he's still preaching on Sunday's down in Old Town Whitehorse."

Jerilyn felt her heart sink, and now her tears were real. She'd come so far, hoping that someone would be able to help her get back on her feet. But she still had Earl Ray's little black book as a last resort, she reminded herself.

"You know if you're afraid about meeting your daughter, we could go together for dinner at the restaurant," Buck suggested. "That way you could see her before you said anything about who you were."

"I don't know." What would be the point now that she knew Maddie's circumstances? Jerilyn took the tissue Buck offered her and dried her tears. So much for her ace in the hole. Just another disappointment.

But she guessed it wouldn't hurt to at least see her daughter. She had come this far. She wouldn't tell Maddie who she was. No reason to. It sounded as if the girl had gone through enough without finding out that her birth mother was no better than her adoptive one.

"You going to be all right?" Buck asked.

She nodded. If her mother hadn't already been dead, Jerilyn would have driven back to Arizona just to confront the old bat.

Shoving down her anger, she rose from bed and headed for the shower, turning to glance back at Buck, who was still sitting on the edge of the bed. "You don't happen to have anything I could wear. Someone stole my clothes out of the back of my car."

If Buck knew she was lying, he didn't let on. She hadn't really expected him to have something she could wear. She was just opening the door to hit him up for money. She'd seen a clothing store on Main Street.

"My sister left some clothes here," Buck said. "She's your size. You're sure welcome to anything that fits."

"Thanks," she said. Hand-me-downs? Nothing was going her way. "You've been great."

Buck grinned bashfully and ducked his head as he went to get the clothing.

Jerilyn stepped into the shower. Was she really going to see her daughter after all these years? It wasn't going to be the reunion she'd hoped for, but she'd hit Buck up for money for dinner and a present for Maddie. She could just leave the gift anonymously at the restaurant.

And then what?

Jerilyn didn't know. She couldn't see herself staying here with Buck. Maybe she could find someone at the bar who had a hankering to go to Vegas. Or she could do something with Earl Ray's little black book.

EARL RAY WAS BETTING he knew Jerilyn, knew her so well he could guess what she'd do next. The woman was predictable, though he had been surprised that she'd taken off on her own.

That wasn't like her. Jerilyn didn't like to think for herself. If he was right, that meant she would already have some man thinking for her. If she didn't, she would soon enough.

That was why the minute Earl Ray had gotten to town, he'd checked out the bars—all six of them. Which one would Jerilyn pick? It was anyone's guess.

He'd thought about asking the bartenders to keep a look out for her and let him know if she showed up.

But Jerilyn had a way of making some men go all protective. He didn't want a well-meaning bartender to warn her that he was asking about her around town. Earl Ray wanted to surprise her.

His plan was to get what she was looking for— Maddie Cavanaugh—and use her as bait to reel back in Jerilyn and his black book.

So, Earl Ray decided to bide his time, stay low to the ground and wait. Wait for Bo Evans to bring him Maddie Cavanaugh.

But he and his two buddies, Bubba and Dude, were holed up in a motel on the edge of town, and his patience was running thin. All Bubba did was complain about Dude, who spent all his time watching television.

Earl Ray wasn't sure how much more of this he could take. If Bo didn't come through—and soon—he was going to have to have another talk with him. Only this time, he might have to let Bubba and Dude work over the slimy bastard.

KATE COULDN'T have been more shocked when she picked up the phone later that evening and heard Chester's voice.

"I think we should talk," he said, sounding as if that was the last thing he wanted to do. "Not on the phone. Meet me at our old place."

There was only one thing they had to talk about. She was trembling inside, a quaking that started at her heart and moved through her bones to ripple across her flesh. Meet at their old place?

"Kate?"

"Yes," she managed to say. "I can be there in thirty minutes."

Chester was silent for a long moment, no doubt remembering the times when they'd had this same conversation. Except back then, they'd both been excited to see each other.

"Fine," he said. "Thirty minutes."

She could hear in his tone how he hated this situation as much as she did.

Kate hung up. She glanced over her shoulder, even though she knew Grayson had driven up to the Loring Colony with Russell to see about buying some pigs from the Hutterites. They would stay for supper. Juanita had gone into town and none of the boys were around.

For a moment, Kate was overwhelmed with guilt. *You have to tell Grayson. You have to tell him everything.*

But she knew she couldn't. Not yet. She was too ashamed. Too afraid of how he would take it.

As she drove to the deserted ranch south of Whitehorse, every instinct told her to turn around, go home and forget the past. But coming back to Montana and the ranch had made that impossible.

The old barn was on a narrow, rutted road. As she came up over a rise in the sprawling grasslands that ran to the horizon, she spotted the weathered structure and was surprised that it looked just as it had all those years ago. Maybe a little more weathered, a few more boards missing, but too much the same.

Her heart did that little jump, and her stomach tensed, remembering the thrill of forbidden love.

She'd loved Chester. Hadn't she? From the beginning, she'd known he wasn't free. That had been part of the allure.

The memory brought a wave of guilt and regret for how cavalier she'd been about sleeping with another woman's husband.

Chester's blue pickup was parked in the shade of the building. As Kate pulled in, she began to quake with a fear that immobilized her.

Chester climbed out of his pickup and stood next to it. In the past, he would have been waiting for her in the barn, in the little secret spot they'd made into a love nest.

She killed her engine and leaving the keys in the ignition, got out. A slight breeze carried the smell of hay and weathering wood.

The scent transported her at rocket speed back to the past. For a moment she had to hold on to the door of her SUV for support. All these years of lying to herself ended in a rush of truth that made her eyes fill with tears.

She swallowed, terrified that she would sob uncontrollably, like she had the last time they had met here.

"I thought we could sit over there out of the sun," Chester said, motioning to an old flatbed pickup that had been abandoned next to the barn.

She nodded wordlessly and, taking a deep breath and

letting it out slowly, followed him. He dusted off a spot for her. The thoughtful gesture was almost her undoing.

"I'm sorry, Kate."

The pain she heard in his voice further weakened her. She sat down on the flatbed and stared out across the open country, remembering how one afternoon they'd danced on the worn wood of the old flatbed trailer while a slow country-and-western song poured out of the speakers in Chester's pick up—the dance as forbidden as their affair.

"I never wanted… I should have…" Chester shook his head as if the words were too hollow to even speak.

"It was a long time ago," she said, not trusting herself to look at him.

"If I had it to do over, I swear I would do it differently," he said, as he sat down next to her.

Easy to say after your marriage ended in divorce, she thought, but held her tongue. There was no rewriting history for either of them.

Kate wet her lips, swallowed the lump in her throat and finally met his gaze. "Have you found out what happened to our baby?"

He shook his head looking miserable.

Why had he asked her out here then? "But you must have some idea how we can find her." It was a local adoption, a secret one. The midwife had known someone who would take care of everything. Unfortunately, she was now deceased.

Chester lowered his head and poked in the dirt with the toe of his boot. "All these years, I wondered if things would have been different if you hadn't lost the baby."

"You wouldn't have left Lila."

He cursed under his breath as he swung his head to look at her, his gaze piercing her. "How do you know that?"

"Because you had made your choice." Her chest hurt as she looked into his eyes. "You could have had me and our baby girl, but you chose Lila and her ranch instead, since I no longer had Trails West."

Kate knew she was being cruel. She blamed him for the way things had turned out. That wasn't fair and she knew it. But even after all these years, she was still angry. Still hurting. She'd given up her baby and had regretted it every day since.

"We were so young," he said quietly.

"Not so young." She'd been twenty-four, old enough that she could have gotten a job and raised her baby on her own.

"It's easy to look back from this age and say that but, Kate, you were in no shape to raise a baby. You'd just lost your father, your home. You'd lost so much, and I let you down." Chester was shaking his head. "You did what you thought best for our baby. You need to forgive yourself."

His kindness brought tears to her eyes again, only this time no amount of willpower could hold them back. Chester knew her better than she'd thought.

"I have to find her." She was crying now, hating that she was. "I have to see her. I have to know that what I did was the right thing."

"Are you sure about this, Kate? What if things didn't work out so well? You'll only have more regrets."

"I shouldn't expect you to understand. You have children. Three daughters."

He nodded. "We adopted. Lila couldn't conceive.

So this daughter of ours is also my only flesh-and-blood child."

Gulping back sobs, she looked into his eyes, saw the pain and the regret.

"Don't you think I hated myself for letting you deal with everything alone? For letting you go?" He reached over and touched her hand.

She flinched, startled by his touch, but didn't pull away. "Will you help me find her?"

He nodded.

"Your daughters are adopted?" She could see that he knew where she was going with this. "Through the same people probably."

"Maybe."

"Lila never knew about you and me or the baby, did she?"

Chester shook his head. Then he let go of her hand and rose to his feet. "Do you want me to call you when I know something?"

"I'll call you." She immediately regretted her words.

Chester's gaze narrowed. "Grayson doesn't know?"

She didn't answer as she got up and walked to her SUV. She made a point of not looking at the barn or remembering the way the sun slanted through the worn wood, warming the straw bed on which her younger self once laid naked in this man's arms.

As Jerilyn stepped into the Northern Lights restaurant that evening, she felt self-conscious and glanced down at her clothing.

Buck had come through with some pretty nice stuff

that fit well. Much better clothes than anything Jerilyn had owned in a long time.

But still she felt nervous. She checked her hair. She'd pulled it up and was glad she did. This place was nice. Her daughter must make good tips.

Jerilyn pushed the thought away as she saw a cute girl come out of the kitchen. Blond, freckled, blue-eyed. Jerilyn felt all the air rush from her lungs and her legs turn to water. This had to be her.

"Will someone be joining you?" the girl asked. Not a girl. A young woman.

Jerilyn swallowed, nodded, then corrected herself. "Just me."

Maddie smiled. "Right this way."

Jerilyn followed, heart pounding, to a table by the window and sat down heavily. Maddie brought her water, a menu and breadsticks.

Jerilyn watched her walk away, then opened the menu, instantly relieved that she'd asked Buck for an extra twenty. He'd also given her the keys to his pickup, which was now parked out front.

Some friends of Buck's had come by to go gopher hunting. She'd insisted he go, telling him she was nervous enough without him hanging around.

After he'd left, she'd watched some television then went through his house looking in all the cubbyholes. For a while she'd pretended he was rich but didn't trust banks. That fairy tale ended when she didn't find anything more than two dollars and twenty-nine cents in spare change.

She'd waited until the last hour and a half before the

restaurant closed before drinking a couple of beers just to get up her courage, then going out. Buck had given her money to buy Maddie a gift, but Jerilyn hadn't made it downtown to look for anything before the stores closed. Not that she would have known what to buy, anyway.

When Maddie returned, Jerilyn ordered three appetizers and a glass of wine and tried to relax.

Only a couple of tables were occupied, the diners at them all about to leave.

She tried to think of something to say to Maddie when she returned with the appetizers.

"Are you from around here?" Jerilyn asked.

"Born and raised," Maddie said with a smile. Jerilyn had always hated her own freckles and wondered if Maddie felt the same about hers. Maddie seemed comfortable in her skin, and Jerilyn was jealous.

"So what is there to do around here?" Jerilyn asked, when Maddie refilled her water glass.

"Well, it depends on what you enjoy. There are two museums, one about the history of the area, the other about dinosaurs." Maddie cocked her head. "You're probably not interested in fishing, right? But there is a hot spring just outside of town if you like to swim or just soak. How long are you planning to be in town? There is a county fair coming up."

Jerilyn couldn't help but laugh. "What do you do here? It doesn't sound like there's much going on."

Maddie smiled at the question. "I spend a lot of time on my horse. But there's always something happening. Last night there was a rodeo and dance…"

"You like it here, then?" Jerilyn hadn't meant to sound so surprised.

It was Maddie's turn to laugh. "I do. I take it this is your first time in Whitehorse."

"My second time," Jerilyn said truthfully. "I'm from Arizona."

"Well, June's a good time to be in Montana. You probably wouldn't like winter here."

"No," Jerilyn agreed. Last time she was in White-horse it hadn't been winter, but she remembered it had felt cold and bleak.

"Let me know if I can get you anything else," Maddie said.

"Thank you. I will." Jerilyn picked at the food, suddenly not hungry. She watched her daughter clear the now-empty tables and heard her humming to herself.

Maddie seemed happy, content, doing okay. What hurt was that Jerilyn could see that her mother had been right. If she had raised this girl, Maddie would have ended up in a foster home or maybe worse, given the type of men she had shacked up with over the years.

She'd always told herself that if she'd kept her baby things would have been different. But as she watched Maddie, she knew she would have been a lousy mother and that her daughter had been better off without her—would always be better off without her. That hurt more than she wanted to admit.

Jerilyn finished her appetizers, paid her bill and left Maddie a large tip. As she stepped outside, her daughter thanked her for coming in and put up the Closed sign behind her.

FINALLY EARL RAY couldn't take it anymore. He decided to leave Bubba and Dude at the motel. The two were scary-looking. Not that Earl Ray was any beauty, but when the three of them were together, they could be mistaken for thugs.

He promised himself that once he got the book and sold it to the highest bidder, he'd buy himself an expensive suit, a nice car and always keep a wad of spending money in his pocket. People would look up to him then. Maybe he'd even find himself a nice woman, a lady. Not another ditz like Jerilyn Larch.

"I'm going to go get myself a beer," Earl Ray told his heavies. He was sure the two had real names, although he'd never asked.

"Whatever." Dude was sprawled on one of the motel beds watching poker on TV.

"Bring me back something to eat," Bubba said from where he was doing push-ups on the floor.

"Sure." Earl Ray already had his story worked out. He'd tell the bartenders that Jerilyn was his sister and their mother was dying. He had to get her back to Arizona before the old gal croaked or Jerilyn would never forgive him.

He hit pay dirt in the third bar.

"Yeah, I saw her," the bartender said after Earl Ray had described Jerilyn. "She was in here last night."

"Do you know where I can find her? Time is of the essence." He'd thrown a twenty-dollar bill down on the bar when he'd ordered a draft beer. He stood now, making it clear he'd be leaving the rest of the twenty as a tip.

"Buck Jones might know. The two of them were talking some last night."

Knowing Jerilyn, she'd gone home with the man. That would explain why he hadn't seen her car at any of the few motels in town.

"Where does he live?"

The bartender hesitated, picked up the twenty, then said, "He lives in a house over by the old high school. Well, where the old high school used to be. It burned down about ten years ago."

Fascinating, Earl Ray thought.

"It's a blue and white place, on the corner."

"You know the name of the street?"

"Fourth. Fourth and Third, I think."

Great directions. Earl Ray thanked him and headed for Buck Jones's house.

AFTER SEEING her daughter, Jerilyn felt restless. Just the thought of going back to Buck's little house was too depressing for words. She walked down the dark street, noting how quiet it was. Why would anyone want to live here? The only sign of life was a few pickups parked in front of the bars on the next block.

One thing was for certain. She couldn't stay in Whitehorse, but she knew Earl Ray's car would never get her back to Arizona—as if there was anything waiting for her there even if the car would make it. Something other than trouble.

She stopped in front of a clothing store and was admiring a spaghetti-strap top in the window, when out of the corner of her eye she saw a set of headlights cut through the darkness. She watched as an older model car pulled up at the corner, motor running. She could see a dark-colored cowboy hat silhouetted against the street lights. The cowboy appeared to be waiting for someone.

The lights inside the Northern Lights restaurant blinked out an instant before the front door opened and Maddie emerged. Jerilyn turned to watch her leave, telling herself it would be the last time she saw her daughter.

Maddie stopped under the eave, hugging herself, as if looking for someone. When she noticed the car parked along the side street, she stepped from under the eave as if to run across the street.

Jerilyn didn't see the cowboy get out of the car. She'd been too busy watching Maddie.

He ran up before Maddie reached the edge of the sidewalk. For a moment, Jerilyn thought it was just Maddie's boyfriend who'd come to pick her up.

Maddie must not have seen or heard the cowboy coming. He grabbed her arm roughly and pulled her toward his waiting car.

Jerilyn watched, frowning, as Maddie didn't seem to want to go with him. Jerilyn opened her mouth to yell at him, taking a couple of steps in their direction.

Maddie was struggling to free herself and digging in her shoulder bag for something. Mace? But before Maddie could get whatever she was after, the cowboy punched her. As she slumped in his arms, he hurriedly dragged her toward the waiting car.

Jerilyn was running now, yelling after him. But the

man didn't turn as he opened the back door of the car and put something over her mouth before he tossed Maddie in. After slamming the door, he leaped into the front seat. The engine revved, and before Jerilyn could reach the corner, the car sped off down the dark street.

She had to call the police. But she had no cell phone. She turned, looking for someone to help. But there was no one, and the closest bar was down the next block.

Racing over to the restaurant door, Jerilyn saw only a dim light in the back. Everyone must have gone home.

Jerilyn turned to look down the street. She could still hear the roar of the cowboy's car as it headed out of town.

Realizing there was nothing else to do, she ran to Buck's pickup. Her fingers trembled as she inserted the key in the ignition and got the motor running. As she whipped out of the parking space and went after her daughter, all Jerilyn could see of the car was the faint red glow of its taillights in the distance.

Chapter Eight

Bo couldn't believe he'd pulled it off. Now he had to find somewhere to pull over and take care of Maddie.

He listened. No sound from the backseat. She was still out, but for how long? He watched his speed. All he needed was to get picked up by the state Highway Patrol.

He just hoped to hell he hadn't overdone the chloroform and killed her. That would take all the fun out of it—not to mention the profit. He had a feeling the men waiting at the motel wanted Maddie alive.

The cell phone Earl Ray gave him vibrated in his jacket pocket. Bo checked and, sure enough, it was from Earl Ray. The guy had left three messages so far today. He must be really anxious to get Maddie. If Earl Ray was that desperate, he would probably pay more for her.

Putting the phone back in his pocket without taking the call, Bo reached into the backseat to hold his hand in front of Maddie's face.

To his relief, he felt her warm breath. Good. He figured he'd deliver her tomorrow. Maybe he'd call

Earl Ray later just to keep the bastard from calling him all the time.

Right now Bo just wanted some time alone with his former fiancée. As much as he didn't want to admit it, he'd never gotten over Maddie. Since she'd left town, there hadn't been anyone else who'd interested him for more than a night or two.

As he turned south on Highway 191, he kicked up his speed to seventy, wishing Montana hadn't done away with its no-speed-limit law—especially up in this part of the state, where there was nothing but open country for miles on end.

He'd had all afternoon to figure out where to take her. Whitehorse gave way to rolling prairie dotted with antelope and cattle. The full moon perched in the starry sky illuminated the countryside, making everything seem surreal as he sped along the open highway.

Bo could see the dark silhouette of the Little Rockies in the distance. It was the only distinguishing feature in the area, a landmark that could be seen for miles. He got a kick out of the fact that Lewis and Clark had thought the mountains were the Rockies and had to rename them the Little Rockies after they found the real thing.

Behind him, Bo noticed a set of headlights. He didn't think too much about it, but he decided to take the back way to the cabin his friend Cody's family had in the Missouri Breaks. He needed to stop and take care of Maddie first, though. She could be coming to at any time. He didn't kid himself that when she regained consciousness she would be hell on wheels.

As the turnoff appeared in his headlights Bo slowed,

noting that the vehicle behind him also braked. He watched in his rearview mirror as the older model pickup turned onto the same road he'd taken.

He still didn't think much of it since he recognized it as belonging to Buck Jones. Buck had a friend who lived down this road. Bo sped up, leaving Buck behind.

Over the next rise, Bo couldn't see the lights from the pickup behind him. He took the first turnoff he found. It dropped down into a coulee of scrub pine. He cut the lights and engine and waited for Buck to go by.

As soon as he saw the pickup disappear down the road, he popped the trunk lid and got out to get the duct tape. Once he had Maddie bound up, she would be all his, he thought with relish.

As he started to dig around in the dark for the duct tape, he heard the worn backseat springs groan.

Bo froze. Maddie was awake.

MADDIE CAME TO slowly. Her cheek hurt, and her head throbbed. At first she didn't know where she was, but as the car rolled over a bump and slowed, it all came back to her.

Bo. She cracked one eye open and saw she was in the back of his car. From where she lay, she was able to see Bo behind the wheel, his Western hat cocked back. From what she could tell, the passenger seat was empty. That was a relief. He was alone.

Without moving, she glanced around for her purse but didn't see it. There was trash on the floorboard and an unpleasant smell that she didn't even want to speculate on.

She didn't dare move as he stopped the car. Closing

her eyes tight, she'd waited. She knew Bo had some-thing in mind. Even if he planned to kill her, he wouldn't do it quickly. That wasn't his style.

She told herself that she had the advantage in that he didn't know she was conscious.

His car door opened and she tensed, expecting him to open the back door to pull her out. Instead, she heard the trunk lid come up. Bo had left the driver's side door open as he walked back to the trunk.

She had to find her purse—and the knife inside it. The dome light was burned out, but the full moon shone into the car.

Fortunately, with the trunk lid up, Bo wouldn't be able to see her. She pushed herself up on one elbow, careful not to make a sound, and spotted her purse. As she listened to him rummaging around in the trunk, Maddie had consid-ered jumping out and running, but she knew she wouldn't stand a chance against Bo. He was strong and fast, and she felt wobbly and weak from what he'd done to her.

No, her best hope was getting to her purse. She raised herself up further and could see it on the floor in front of the passenger seat. The flap on the shoulder bag was open. Had Bo found the steak knife? Or had the bag come open during the struggle?

If she could get the knife without Bo hearing her…

"MADDIE'S MISSING."

"What?" Shane blinked and fought to wake up. The phone had dragged him up out of the nightmare that had haunted his sleep for months. He glanced at the clock beside his bed. Just past eleven. "Jud? What in the—"

"Maddie. I've tried to locate her from here, but it's impossible, and even if I left right now, I couldn't get there fast enough, not if—"

"Whoa." Shane sat up in the bed, some of the dark fog of the dream burning off. "I'm not getting in the middle of this long-distance romance again. Stop leading this woman on." Shane started to hang up.

"Shane, no one has seen Maddie since she left the restaurant at about nine-thirty tonight. Her pickup is still parked across the street. She never made it home."

He heard real concern in his brother's voice.

"Her cousins are afraid something has happened to her," Jud continued. "The sheriff has a deputy out looking for her, but that country is so huge. She could be anywhere."

Shane groaned as he swung his feet over the side of the bed, the phone still at his ear. He couldn't help thinking about Bo Evans.

"Maybe a friend picked her up and she lost track of time."

"She would have called," Jud said. "The cousins are worried about some old boyfriend of hers. They say he's trouble. Shane, I'm afraid she's in danger. I know she's all wrong for me and me for her. But damn it, Shane, I don't want to see anything happen to her."

Shane swore under his breath.

"Please. You're trained in this sort of thing. I know if anyone can find her, you can. I promise I'll break it off as soon as I know she's all right. Just find her and make sure she's okay. That's all I ask."

"That's all you ask?" Shane said and swore. "Just

give me the information." He wrote down the cousins' names and numbers. He already knew what Bo drove.

"The one cousin, Laci, lives over the restaurant with her husband, Bridger. Unfortunately, neither of them heard anything or saw her lock up and leave."

"I'll see what I can do." He hung up. Shane was even more worried than Jud. He'd met Bo Evans. If Bo had Maddie, then God help her.

JERILYN TOPPED another hill. No sign of the car's red tail-lights. Was it possible he'd turned off? She had tried to stay back far enough that the cowboy wouldn't see she was following him. Now she realized that had been a mistake.

She thought about turning around and going back, but she had no idea which of the turnoffs he might have taken, so she kept going, thinking he might still be ahead of her.

The horizon filled with the dark fringe of pine trees. One of the roads headed up the side of the hill. She could see the bare bones of a house under construction. There were no lights on, no vehicles around. She turned in.

Her headlights moved across the grayed wood of an abandoned house. She turned around and noticed that she had a good view of the road she'd come down. He had to be behind her. He'd pulled off. Probably afraid she was following him. Maybe if she waited…

Jerilyn cut her lights, telling herself turning off had been impulsive and crazy—just like her. But from here she could see the road both to the north and south.

If she was right, he'd be coming up that road soon.

She refused to think about what would happen if she was wrong. The bastard had her daughter. She couldn't let that man hurt her daughter, could she?

While she waited, Jerilyn realized that Maddie's cousins were bound to get worried when the girl didn't return home. They'd call the sheriff. The whole county would be looking for Maddie Cavanaugh.

Everyone would think she'd been kidnapped.

Maybe that was why the cowboy had grabbed Maddie. No, the way he'd taken her looked more personal than financial. From what Jerilyn could tell, Maddie had known him. And anyway, there wasn't any ransom money to get, right?

But Jerilyn couldn't help wondering what the owners of that nice restaurant might pay to get Maddie back.

It was just a random thought, she told herself. Just something to amuse herself while she waited. Kidnap her own daughter? What a crazy thought.

BO FOUND THE DUCT TAPE and stood listening for the springs to groan again. Maybe Maddie had just stirred. It would take her a while to really come to, wouldn't it? And if she was conscious, wouldn't she have tried to get away by now?

He couldn't be sure. This Maddie was different from the one to whom he'd been engaged.

"Maddie Cavanaugh's all wrong for you," his mother had told him time and time again. "I know her mother and I've heard things about Maddie. Believe me, the girl's got some head problems. You don't want to be taking that on. A woman like that, you never know what she'll do."

Not that he ever paid any attention to his mother's advice. He'd seen how Arlene's life had gone, and he had no plan to mess his up in the same way. He wanted no part of farming, ranching or work of any kind. Nor did he really want to get married.

He'd only asked Maddie to marry him because he couldn't stand the thought of any other man being with her—and he'd stolen the engagement ring for her.

Now Maddie had changed. And so had his mother. Bo still couldn't believe that his own mother had put him out of the house. He'd once been her favorite. He could do nothing wrong. And then Arlene had met some stupid man and turned on her only son.

"You're twenty-five, Bo," she'd said the last time he'd seen her. "Do something with your life. Don't waste it. If there is one thing I've learned, it's that you're never too old to change. I'm doing this for your own good. Someday you'll thank me."

Bo had laughed. "When hell freezes over," he'd told her, enjoying the hurt he'd seen in her eyes.

But she hadn't relented, and he hated her for it just as he hated Maddie for what she'd done to him.

Bo realized he should have brought a flashlight. There used to be one in the trunk, but the batteries would probably be shot. He felt around, his hand brushing cool plastic. The flashlight. He tested it, putting his palm over the light end. If Maddie was playing possum, he was about to find out.

As he started to slam the trunk, he stopped himself. Cautiously, he moved around the side of the car. The backseat was in shadow, too dark to see if she was awake and just lying there waiting. He felt the hair rise on the back of his neck as he reached for the back-door handle on the passenger side—the side closest to her pretty little head.

MADDIE HAD HEARD the groan of the seat springs as she'd retrieved the knife from her purse, and she feared Bo had, too.

Lying back down, she curled around the steak knife and waited, her blood thrumming in her veins.

The door by her head suddenly swung open. She felt the cold night breeze rustle her hair, but she willed herself not to move.

She could feel Bo standing over her, staring down at her. She felt dirty just thinking of the way he would be looking at her.

She heard a snap and almost flinched as she sensed a flashlight beam flicker over her. She held her breath, anticipating his touch.

Still, when his warm palm brushed her shoulder, she winced. He must not have felt it, because his free hand moved over her shoulder and slowly down her arm as the dim flashlight beam wavered a little.

His hand slowed, then brushed across her left breast. Revulsion washed over her as his hand cupped her breast and squeezed.

It was all Maddie could do not to pull the knife and go for his throat. But she knew he had her at a disadvantage. With him behind her like he was, she knew he could see it coming. She had to wait.

He lifted his hand from her breast and the flashlight

beam blinked out. With a groan, the door slammed shut. She had expected him to try to rape her. Now she didn't know what to think.

The other passenger door suddenly opened and Maddie heard a sound that took her only an instant to recognize.

Tape being ripped off a roll.

She knew it was now or never as he grabbed her ankles.

SHANE DROVE through the moonlit night toward White-horse, telling himself that Maddie would probably turn up before he reached the city limits.

There was no traffic on the road at this hour. The moon was huge as it hung in the sky.

He hoped Maddie had just gone off with a friend, but every instinct told him it wasn't something Maddie would do without letting her family know.

Whitehorse was dead. There were just a couple of vehicles in front of the only bar still open at this hour on a weekday night. Down the street, there was a lone pickup parked across from the Northern Lights restaurant. Maddie's.

Shane parked and walked across the street to circle the truck. To his relief he saw no sign of a struggle near the truck: no blood, no scuff marks, no spilled contents of a purse.

Cupping his hands over his eyes, he looked inside the cab. Nothing out of the ordinary. Covering his hand with his sleeve, he tried the door. Locked.

As he glanced toward the front door to the restaurant, he saw the light on inside and the woman waiting anxiously for him.

She unlocked the door as he neared. "Are you Shane?"

He nodded.

"I'm Laci Cavanaugh Duvall, Maddie's cousin."

Shane took her hand. It was ice cold. "You called the sheriff?"

She nodded. "My brother-in-law, Deputy Nick Giovanni, is out looking for Maddie. So is my husband, Bridger."

"Do they know about Bo Evans?"

She scowled. "Everyone knows about Bo Evans."

"Bo's been harassing Maddie lately. Did she tell you that?"

"She never said a word," Laci said, shaking her head and looking close to tears. "She said she saw him but that was all."

"Is it possible she went off with him?"

"No! She'd never go near him."

"They used to be engaged, I heard."

"That was a long time ago," Laci said. "For a while, Maddie was under his spell. Or should I say under his thumb?"

"Maybe she's fallen under it again."

Laci shook her head adamantly. "Bo abused her. She was going through something, and he took advantage of her vulnerability. But Maddie isn't that girl anymore. She's strong and determined. She'd never go back to Bo, and he knows it."

Shane liked Laci's conviction, but he also knew that sometimes people got caught up in things that were bad for them. He couldn't help but think of Kate and wonder what she was caught up in.

"We need to find out where Bo is," Shane said. "Your brother-in-law needs to question him right away."

"I was hoping Maddie was with your brother, Jud," Laci said. "I thought maybe he had come down from his movie shoot to surprise her."

"She's not with Jud."

"I know. I guess I just can't stand the thought that she might be with Bo," Laci said. "Jud said you were a Texas Ranger. Can you help find her?"

He didn't tell her that he was on a medical leave or that he didn't feel up to this. If Maddie was in trouble, she needed someone who wasn't wounded both physically and emotionally.

Instead, Shane said, "I'll try. Can you get hold of your brother-in-law? Maybe he's already found Bo."

Laci pulled out her cell phone and stepped away for a moment, her free hand resting on the baby she carried inside her.

Shane couldn't bear the thought that Maddie might never know her niece or nephew—or vice versa.

"Nick has been looking for Bo," Laci said after she got off the phone. "The problem is Bo no longer has a permanent residence here. But Nick heard that three men driving a car with Arizona plates have been asking about how to find Bo. He's looking into that."

Shane thought of the two men he'd seen Bo with the night of the rodeo dance. They'd apparently found him.

"What about Bo's friends?"

"He has only one that I know of—Cody Barnes. He lives in a trailer over by the river," Laci said. "But I'm sure Nick has already talked to him."

"It won't hurt to talk to him again," Shane said, then asked for the directions to Cody's place and Laci's cell-phone number.

As he left, Shane looked to the table where he'd had lunch earlier that day. He recalled the way the sunshine had streamed into the room from the front window and set fire to Maddie's hair. She had more red in her blond hair than her cousin. More fire in her than maybe any of them knew.

He could only hope that was true because he feared tonight Maddie might need all the strength she could muster.

MADDIE ROSE up from the backseat of Bo's car, lunging as she thrust the knife. At the last second, she pulled to the right, unable to put the blade into another human being's heart. But the blade connected with flesh, and as Bo shrieked, she recoiled in horror at what she'd done.

"You bitch!" Bo screamed. A dark stain blossomed across his shirtsleeve, where she'd stabbed his upper arm. He stumbled backward into the darkness. "You crazy bitch! *You stabbed me!*"

With momentum still carrying her forward, Maddie stumbled from the car, dropping to one knee in the dirt, the knife in her hand. As Bo started to lunge for her, she brandished the knife to keep him back, still shocked by what she'd done.

"Are you friggin' crazy?" Bo demanded. He had dropped the flashlight at his feet. The beam cut a swath of pale light in his direction. He held up both hands in surrender, but Maddie wasn't fooled.

She knew that if he got the knife away from her, he'd use it on her. With relief, she saw that he didn't seem to be badly hurt. She'd only managed to make him more angry. But he was also scared of her, she saw, and realized she could use that to get away from him.

"Damn, Maddie, why did you have to go and do that?" he asked, sounding as shocked as she was that she'd actually cut him.

"This from the man who abducted me and nearly broke my jaw?" She abhorred violence, and yet here she was with a bloody steak knife in her hand.

She wanted to cry but knew if she did, Bo would see it as a sign of weakness. She held the knife in front of her, forcing him back another step.

"What else was I to do but kidnap you? You wouldn't talk to me. All I wanted to do was talk to you."

"I don't want to talk you. I never wanted to see you again. Wasn't that clear enough?" Her anger scared her. She was shaking, still appalled that she'd stabbed him.

"How can you say that?" he whined. "I loved you."

She shook her head. "That wasn't love."

"Like you know all about love?" he said, getting angry again as he grabbed his upper arm and winced in pain. "You stabbed me!"

Maddie had seen that the car keys were still in the ignition. She edged backward to slam the car door and saw Bo tense.

"What are you doing, Maddie?" he asked warily.

She didn't answer as she moved toward the back of the car.

"I don't blame you for being a little upset with me,

but you need to get me to a doctor. I'm going to bleed to death if you don't."

She said nothing as she slammed the trunk, keeping the knife so he could see it.

"Maddie, you know how I am," he whined. "If you had just talked to me…"

She edged around the car. "Stay where you are."

He nodded as though the idea of coming after her had never crossed his mind.

She knew once she got behind the wheel, she would have to move quickly. It worried her that Bo seemed to be giving up so easily. It wasn't like him.

At the open driver-side door, she glanced at him over the roof of the car. He was standing where she'd left him, which surprised her.

"You're just going to leave me out here to die?" he asked, his voice laced with fury.

When she and Bo were together, his mood swings used to scare her. Watching him now, she was even more terrified by how quickly he could change. She knew if she didn't get away from him tonight, he would hurt her. Hurt her bad.

She ducked into the car, slammed the door and hit the door locks as she reached for the key in the ignition.

To her shock, the passenger-side door flew open as the engine turned over, and belatedly she realized why Bo had stayed where he was. He'd known that the locks didn't work.

She shifted the car into First and hit the gas, but Bo managed to get in. The flashlight hit her in the side of the face and knocked her against the window. Stunned by the blow, her foot came up off the gas pedal, the car lurching forward.

Bo was on her before she could get control again. He grabbed the steering wheel with one hand and harshly twisted the knife from her hand with the other.

Pinning her against the driver-side door, he shut off the engine and slammed his foot down on the brake. The car came to a jarring stop, throwing her forward into the steering wheel.

His hands were on her throat as he banged her head against the door window and screamed obscenities.

Maddie felt her eyes bulge, her throat rasping as she frantically tried to fight him off and breathe.

"Stupid bitch. Stupid damned bitch," Bo cursed, his eyes wild with rage.

She felt blackness encroaching on her vision. Her hand found the door handle, but to her disappointment, the door refused to open. Unlike the passenger-side door, this one had locked.

As she felt herself slipping away, her other hand reached for Bo. She raked her fingernails down his face, determined to fight him till the brutal end.

EARL RAY PITTS didn't believe in coincidences. When he'd gone by Buck Jones's house, he'd found his stolen car in the drive, but no sign of Jerilyn—or Buck Jones.

When he'd tried to get hold of Bo Evans, the little bastard didn't answer.

Something was up. Earl Ray could feel it.

"Let's go," he told Dude and Bubba when he got

back at the motel. He grabbed the remote control and shut off the television. "What's your problem, Dude? Don't you have cable TV at home?"

"Hey, I'm going to miss one of my favorite shows."

"What did you bring me to eat?" Bubba asked.

Earl Ray tossed him a bag of chips from the vending machine outside and headed for the door.

"Where are we going?" Dude asked as they followed.

"We're going to find Bo Evans." He didn't tell Dude that the cell phone he gave Bo had a GPS on it. The phone and Bo Evans were to the south in what was called the Missouri Breaks. As for Jerilyn—who the hell knew where that broad was?

Earl Ray climbed in the passenger side of the rented SUV and ordered Dude to drive south. Bubba slid into the back.

As they left Whitehorse, Earl Ray couldn't help but think about the first time he'd laid eyes on Jerilyn. She'd been sitting at a bar, playing with a lock of her blond hair the way teenagers do. She'd seemed young and exciting.

It wasn't until later he realized she was neither. She was a woman trapped in the past. A girl who never grew up. Earl Ray hadn't understood it until he'd seen the note in her purse. He was no psychiatrist, but he'd put his money on her problems having something to do with the baby she gave up.

"I thought we were looking for Jerilyn," Dude said, as they left town and the country began to change.

"Just drive and try not to think." His instincts had

kept him alive this long. For Earl Ray that was good enough. He'd been right about Jerilyn coming to Montana. He knew he would be right about Bo Evans.

JERILYN MUST HAVE dozed. She sat up with a start, blinded by a set of headlights coming up the hill on the other road. For a moment, she thought she was still on the way to Montana.

Automatically she hunkered down in the seat, even though she was sure the driver of the car wouldn't notice the pickup parked beside the abandoned house.

The car drove past, silhouetted in the moonlight. The cowboy and his old junker. He wasn't wearing his hat, she noted. Nor was there any sign of Maddie as the car disappeared over the rise.

Was it possible he'd left Maddie back up the road?

Jerilyn doubted it. She was all too familiar with men like the one who'd grabbed her daughter. They dealt in meanness and pain. It was what they knew, what they reveled in. The man who'd grabbed Maddie had some reason he'd chanced taking her off the street. He wouldn't have dumped her that quickly. No, a man like that wouldn't be finished with her already. She was putting her money on Maddie still being in that car. Otherwise, wouldn't the cowboy have gone back toward town?

Jerilyn waited a few heartbeats, then started the pickup. The moon seemed brighter now. She could make out shapes even in the distance. The cowboy would get suspicious if her headlights suddenly showed up in his rearview mirror again. She'd have to drive without lights and remember not to touch her brakes.

Tentatively she pulled back onto the road. With the moon high and bright, it was almost like daylight. She sped up as her confidence grew. Over the next rise, she saw the cowboy's taillights and, keeping them in view, followed at a safe distance.

As she drove, Jerilyn let her mind wander. It circled back to an earlier thought, one that had nagged at her until she had fallen asleep. *What was in this for her?* She could be risking her life. Shouldn't she get something other than gratitude and maybe her name and photo in the paper for saving Maddie?

It didn't seem fair. She was flat broke and needed all the help she could get. The rest of the world had been so much luckier in life than her.

"Buck won't call the sheriff right away," Jerilyn said aloud, working out the details as she drove under the vast canopy of the Big Sky. "He'll be a little concerned about his pickup. After all, he is a man. But he won't call the sheriff. Not with my car sitting in front of his house. He trusts me—or at least wants to. He'll wait a day or two. Maybe more since he's the kind of man who still has faith in women. The fool."

Ahead, Jerilyn saw the taillights glow brighter as the cowboy hit his brakes. She didn't dare touch her own. Shifting down, she slowed the pickup as the car ahead of her turned off onto a narrow road and disappeared.

She coasted to a stop up the road from where he'd turned off and pulled over in a stand of pines. Cutting the engine, she rolled down her window. The only sound was the tick of the pickup's engine as it cooled.

As she dropped open the glove box, Jerilyn let out a pleased cry of surprise before she carefully pulled out the pistol.

She'd known Buck was practical. Organized, too, it seemed, because behind the .22 was a full box of ammunition.

THE TAPE AROUND Maddie's wrists and ankles was cutting off her circulation. She had tried not to panic at having the duct tape over her mouth. When Bo had finally stopped choking her, she'd gasped for breath, her throat on fire and her lungs crying out for oxygen.

He'd held her down, taping first her wrists, then her ankles, all the time his weight painfully pressing her down.

"Bo, think about what you're doing," she'd said, trying to reason with him even though she knew it was futile. "No good can come of this."

He'd slapped a piece of tape over her mouth. She was filled with terror at the thought of what Bo would do with her now. He'd crossed some line and they both knew it.

As the car rolled to a stop, Maddie saw a wall of dark pines outside the window. The front seat creaked. She heard Bo sigh. Was he starting to realize how foolish this had been?

The driver-side door let out a tortured groan as it opened. Maddie felt a shaft of even colder night air rush in and braced herself.

The back car door opened. She closed her eyes, not wanting to even look at him. Her face hurt from where he'd hit her, first with his fist and then with the flashlight. Her throat felt raw and bruised, and it was all she could do to fight back tears of both pain and fear.

She no longer had any doubt about the seriousness of her situation. The flashlight had split the skin over her right eye. She could still taste the blood and feel it clotted on her cheek and eyelashes. But at least it was no longer running down into her eye and blinding her.

She fought for calm. Bo fed off fear, and she didn't need to give him any more reason to hurt her.

As she felt his hands slip under her shoulders, she tried not to recoil at his touch. He dragged her out and stood her up, leaning her against the side of the car as he bent to bring his shoulder up under her, then carried her like a sack of potatoes.

She caught sight of a small, dark cabin and realized she should have known where he would bring her. Just the sight of the cabin triggered memories of the times Bo had brought her here when they'd been engaged. The cabin was isolated and seldom used. No phone. Miles from another human being. Maddie willed herself not to think about that now. Bo would want her to panic and try to get away.

At the door to the cabin, he stood her up against the wall. She watched him feel around on the ledge for the key, praying someone in the Barnes family had moved it and realizing as he found the key that it wouldn't have mattered. Bo would have simply broken a window to get in.

As he unlocked and opened the door, Maddie watched, knowing she stood no chance against him with her ankles and wrists bound.

A light blinked on inside, and Bo was in front of her again. Their eyes met for an instant, and Maddie cringed at the sick anticipation she saw there.

Lifting her, he carried her inside and dropped her unceremoniously on a weathered, old couch. She strained against the tape as she heard him go back out to the car, pop the trunk again, then slam it shut. What could he have gone back for?

Her question was answered moments later when he returned to sit down on the edge of the coffee table in front of the couch.

Her heart dropped at the sight of what he held in his hands. Hedge trimmers. The blades were long and shiny, and they looked sharp as razors.

A small sound of terror escaped from behind her taped mouth as Bo reached down and grabbed her blouse, ripping it open.

Smiling, he slipped one cold, thin blade under the front of her bra. "Snip, snip," he said, and snapped the blades closed, cutting her bra and exposing her breasts.

Chapter Nine

As Shane was leaving the Northern Lights restaurant, he noticed a man coming down the street. What caught his eye was the way the man was looking at Maddie's truck.

The man drew closer, then started to turn around and go back the way he'd come.

"Just a minute!" Shane called out as he strode down the sidewalk to him.

"Yes?" The man was in his fifties, wearing worn jeans and boots and a canvas jacket that was stained with blood left over from hunting season. Or grease. Or both.

"I noticed you're interested in that pickup," Shane said motioning to Maddie's truck.

The man laughed, sounding embarrassed. "I thought it was mine. Same year. Looked like the same color from a distance."

"You've lost your truck?" It was clear that the man had had a few drinks, but he didn't appear drunk enough to have lost his pickup.

"My girlfriend borrowed it to go out to dinner." He squinted at Shane. "I don't think I've seen you around."

"Shane Corbett. I'm staying out at the—"

"Trails West Ranch," the man said, nodding and smiling. "You must be the son who's a Texas Ranger, the one who got shot." He grinned. "Noticed you limping a little. Name's Buck Jones." He extended his hand. "Sorry, but there are no secrets in a town this size."

"I guess not," Shane said with a laugh, although he disagreed. Everyone had secrets, and small towns hoarded them. "You say your girlfriend borrowed your truck?"

"My girlfriend. I guess you could call her that," he said, smiling shyly. "I was a little worried about her. I could see how nervous she was." Buck seemed to notice Shane's questioning look. "She was going to meet her daughter at the restaurant. Her daughter waitresses there."

Shane's ears perked up. "Which waitress is that?"

"Maddie Cavanaugh."

"I thought Maddie's mother wasn't around here anymore." Hadn't Jud told him there was bad blood between Maddie and her mother?

Buck was shaking his head. "Not that mother. Jerilyn, the woman who has my truck, is Maddie's birth mother."

"Maddie was adopted?" Jud hadn't mentioned this.

"Apparently so," Buck said. "Jerilyn gave her up at birth and hadn't seen her since. She was going to the restaurant to introduce herself. I wanted to go with her, but she said she had to do it alone."

Shane couldn't believe what he was hearing. This definitely put a whole new spin on things. "Then you don't know if this Jerilyn…"

"Larch. Jerilyn Larch from Arizona."

Arizona? "You don't know if she told her daughter who she was?"

Buck shook his head. "I hope things went as she'd wanted."

"Your truck isn't the only thing missing," Shane said. "No one has seen Maddie since she left the restaurant tonight. Her cousins are worried about her. I think you'd better talk to the sheriff. His deputy, Nick Giovanni, is out looking for Maddie. If Jerilyn and Maddie are together…"

Buck nodded his head. "I'll give the dispatcher a call and have Nick be on the lookout for my pickup. They probably just went for a ride together to talk."

Shane wished he believed that.

THE WALK to the turnoff where Jerilyn had seen the car disappear didn't take her but a few minutes. At the mouth of the narrow side road stood a pine tree with a small wooden sign tacked to it.

She had to step closer to read it. *Barnes.* The road into the Barneses' place looked as if no one had been here for a while. Grass grew ankle deep, and there was only the one set of tracks in the dust from where the cowboy's car had gone in.

Jerilyn hadn't walked far up the road when she saw a light glowing through the pines. A little farther and she saw the bastard's beat-up old car.

She caught her breath and rubbed her knee, which she'd scraped when she fell down just moments before on the road in to the cabin. Her hand was also scraped and bleeding, and she felt a little nauseous now that she was here, since she didn't have any kind of a plan.

Inching toward the light burning in the cabin, Jerilyn figured she'd take a look in the window and then decide what to do.

As she passed the car, she had a thought. The moonlight glimmered off the keys dangling from the ignition. Jerilyn eased the car door open, cringing at the sound it made.

Her thought had been to start the engine. The cowboy would come running out, and Maddie could get away. But as Jerilyn began to slide behind the wheel, she spotted the knife on the driver-side floorboard. Picking it up, she saw a smear of blood on the blade and quickly dropped it.

"Oh hell," she whispered, as she looked toward the house. Her pulse began to pound when she realized that Maddie might not be able to escape on her own.

Jerilyn pulled the keys from the ignition, pocketed them and slid back out, leaving the car door open so that the noise of closing it wouldn't call attention to her. She shivered as she moved toward the cabin, aware that this might be the craziest thing she'd ever done.

But her baby girl was in there.

And Maddie's great aunt and uncle would be so happy if Jerilyn saved her from this bastard.

Pulling the .22 from her pocket, she wondered just how grateful they would be. Enough that they'd at least buy her a bus ticket out of town.

She couldn't hear any sounds coming from the cabin, but she wasn't taking any chances. At the window, she leaned against the side of the log building to catch her breath. The higher altitude was killing her. That and the lousy condition she was in from years of boozing, smoking and bad eating habits.

After a few moments, she slid closer to the window and peered in through a crack in the curtain. Her fingers tightened on the gun in her hand.

The cowboy stood over Maddie, who lay bound and gagged on a couch in the center of the room, her shirt open. He held what looked like hedge trimmers and was snapping the blades in the air over Maddie's bare breasts.

Jerilyn thought of all the men she'd known who seemed just like this one. Seeing her daughter's terrified expression, she felt sick to her stomach as she gripped the .22 and edged toward the door.

SHANE CALLED LACI from his truck. "Was Maddie the only waitress working at the restaurant tonight?"

"Yes."

"Did you see her after her last customer left?" he asked.

"I came back down for a minute earlier. Why?"

"Did she seem upset?" Shane asked.

"No, and I would have been able to tell. Why? Did one of the customers give her a hard time or something?"

Shane repeated the description Buck had given him of Jerilyn Larch and asked if Laci knew if Maddie had waited on the woman.

"Now that you mention it, I remember there was a woman who fits that description," Laci said. "She ordered three appetizers just before closing. I glanced out from the kitchen, a little surprised that the woman was alone."

So she was alone. "Did you see Maddie talking to her?"

"Yes."

"Is there any chance Maddie might have left with her?"

"*What?* Why would Maddie do that? I'm sure she didn't know her. She wasn't local. Why are you asking me all these questions about this woman?"

Shane rubbed a hand over his face. "Was Maddie adopted?"

"*Adopted?* No, of course not."

"You know that for a fact?"

"No, I mean, I remember my aunt had a hard pregnancy. She had to have a lot of bed rest so we didn't see much of her."

He could hear Laci wavering. "It's possible that this Jerilyn Larch might have told Maddie that she was her birth mother."

"*What?* Is that true?"

"I don't know. What would Maddie have done?" he asked.

"I…I don't know. Maddie's been through so much." Laci was crying. "Where is this woman?"

"Apparently she and the pickup she borrowed are also missing but the sheriff's department has been notified. They're looking for the pickup she was driving."

"You think Maddie might be with her?" Laci asked.

"Maybe. I'm going over to Buck's now. Apparently Jerilyn Larch left her car at his house. I'm hoping there is something in it to give us a clue where the woman has gone."

BO EVANS FELT the cell phone vibrate in his pocket. This was the fourth time in a matter of minutes, and it was getting damned annoying.

Worried that something might have happened to change Earl Ray's mind about the deal they'd made, Bo swore and laid the hedge clippers on the coffee table in front of the couch.

He stroked a hand over Maddie's bare breasts, pinching a nipple, before he reached into his pocket and took out the phone. Bo figured he'd keep the phone after this was over. He couldn't afford one of his own. Hell, he could hardly afford gas for his old beater car.

The messages were all the same. Except for the last one. "Listen, you sniveling little bastard. You stop whatever the hell it is you're doing and call me. *Now.* If I don't hear from you, I'm going to come looking for you. You don't want that to happen—trust me."

Bo wanted to tell Earl Ray to take a flying leap, but he needed the money the man had promised him. All he had to do was give him Maddie, which he intended to do. First thing in the morning.

"I gotta take this, sweetheart," he said to Maddie. "Don't worry, I won't be long—and then we can have some fun. I know you can't wait." He laughed as he left the room. No reason to let Maddie know what he had planned for her with Earl Ray.

In the back room, he hit speed dial. Earl Ray thought of everything. The man answered on the first ring.

"Why the hell haven't you been answering my calls?"

"I've been a little busy," Bo said, trying to keep his voice down. "You want Maddie, don't you?"

"What are you saying? That you have her?"

"That's right."

"Then why haven't you called?"

Bo looked to the ceiling. He wanted to say, "I'm not ready to hand her over yet." Instead, he said, "I was thinking of renegotiating the deal we made, since it seems you want her pretty bad."

"You should give that some thought."

"I have. Double the money and I'll bring her to you tomorrow morning."

"If you have her, why not deliver her tonight?"

Bo considered. "Because I already have her, but I'm not in town. It has to be in the morning or no deal."

"You really are a stupid bastard," Earl Ray said.

"Hey, no name calling or the deal is off." Bo held his breath, afraid for a moment that Earl Ray had hung up on him. "You want her, up the ante."

"Tomorrow morning. But leave your phone on. Don't make me leave any more messages."

Bo heard something in the man's voice that told him Earl Ray wasn't bluffing. He was anxious to get back to Maddie, but, he reminded himself, they had all night. This time tomorrow, he'd be in the money after a fulfilling night with his former fiancée. Life didn't get any better than this.

"You can have Maddie at ten."

"Let's make it eight. I'm tired of waiting."

Eight? That still gave Bo plenty of time with Maddie. "Sure, why not?"

JERILYN HAD WAITED until she saw the cowboy put down the hedge trimmers to check his cell phone and then leave the room.

On the couch, Maddie strained to loosen the tape binding her. She managed to get into a sitting position, glancing over her shoulder toward the back of the cabin.

Jerilyn could only assume by the frantic way Maddie worked that she could hear the man talking on the cell phone and knew she didn't have much time left before he came back.

Now or never, Jerilyn thought, as she reached for the doorknob and turned it. She slipped inside, closing the door quietly behind her. She could hear the man in a room at the back talking quietly on the phone.

The couch was only a few steps away, but Jerilyn was afraid the floor would creak or that the man would finish his call too quickly.

As she stepped carefully in front of the couch, Maddie looked up, and her eyes widened in shock. Jerilyn pressed a finger to her lips, her gaze going to the hallway that led to the room where the man was still on the phone.

Maddie's gaze flicked from Jerilyn's face to the .22 gripped in her hand. Jerilyn hurriedly pocketed the gun and picked up the hedge trimmers from the coffee table.

Moving to Maddie, she opened the trimmers and worked the blades between the girl's taped ankles.

The tape was thick, and it took a few moments before she could cut through it. Maddie held up her bound hands behind her, trying to pull the tape apart so Jerilyn could get the blades between them. As the tape sliced apart, Maddie reached at once for the duct tape across her mouth.

Jerilyn touched her fingers to her own lips in warning.

Maddie nodded in understanding, then ripped off the tape and got to her feet. Jerilyn showed her the car keys she'd taken, and Maddie nodded again.

As they headed for the door, Jerilyn pulled the .22 from her pocket. Maddie, she noticed, had picked up the hedge trimmers and tried to cover her nakedness before making her way out the door.

SHANE WALKED AROUND the old Buick with the Arizona plates once before he opened the unlocked passenger-side door. The car's old-dirty-socks smell rose to his nostrils and he grimaced. From what he could tell, Jerilyn Larch had been living in the car.

His worry increased as he opened the glove box and took out the car registration. The Buick was registered to an Earl Ray Pitts of Bullhead City, Arizona.

Had she borrowed the car? Stolen it? And where was Mr. Pitts? He thought about the two men he'd seen with Bo Evans. Definitely not from Whitehorse.

Unfortunately, he found nothing in the car to help him locate Jerilyn or Earl Ray Pitts. As he was leaving, he called the sheriff's department, and the dispatcher put him through to Nick. Shane passed along what he knew to the deputy, including the plate number on the car.

"Any luck turning up Bo Evans?" he asked the deputy.

"Unfortunately, no. Bo's bad news. You still think Maddie's with him? What about this woman who claims to be her mother?"

"Either way I don't think Maddie left of her own free will."

"I checked with Bo's mother," Nick said. "She hasn't seen him. He isn't staying with her. She made that pretty clear. And his friend Cody swears he hasn't seen him."

Shane turned down a side road. Cody Barnes's trailer appeared in the pickup's headlights. "I'm on my way to talk to Cody myself. You have my cell number. Call me if you hear anything."

Shane disconnected as he pulled into the drive and cut his lights. A beat-up SUV sat in front of the lit-up trailer.

As he walked up to the trailer, Shane heard the throb of loud music. He didn't bother to knock. He just swung open the door catching Cody by surprise.

Cody wore a knitted skull cap down to his eyes, worn jeans and a dirty, oversized sweatshirt with Got A Quarter? across the front.

Shane strode to the boom box and yanked out the cord, sending the trailer into a sudden deafening silence.

"What the hell?" Cody yelled.

He was standing in front of the stove, a spatula in his hand and what smelled like hamburger sizzling in a skillet in front of him.

"I'm looking for Bo Evans," Shane said.

"He's not here. I already told the deputy that. Who the hell are you?"

"Shane Corbett. Bo's been staying with you, right?" He asked, stepping down the hall past two clothes-strewn bedrooms.

"He had no place to go, so I said he could stay for a while." Cody sounded defensive. "But I haven't seen him tonight, okay?" The burger in the skillet began to burn.

"If Bo isn't planning to stay here tonight, where would he go?"

"Beats me." Cody looked as if he'd been at the bar earlier tonight.

"You just told me that Bo's options are so limited that he's staying with you. Where would he go if he wanted to be alone with his girlfriend?"

"Maddie?" Cody looked shocked. He shut off the burner and moved the skillet off to one side. "They're back together?"

"Why wouldn't they be?"

"Are you kidding? She dumped him, said she never wanted to see him again."

"Maybe that's why Maddie's cousins are worried about her and asked me to find her. Where would Bo take her so they could be completely alone? If you know where he is and don't tell me and he does something to Maddie—"

Cody's expression changed. "He used to take her to my folks' cabin down in the Breaks. I'm sure he still knows where we hide the key."

GRAYSON WOKE to find the spot next to him in the bed empty. He glanced at the clock, saw how late it was and went to find his wife.

He found Kate standing in the living room staring out into the night. Her slim body was silhouetted against the night sky, her shoulders slumped, her head down, her fingers pressed against the glass.

For so long, he'd turned away. Pretended nothing was wrong. He'd given her space, praying she would come to him when she was ready.

But Grayson realized he could no longer do that. He loved this woman. She was in obvious pain, and he couldn't let her suffer alone any longer.

As he stepped toward her, he feared she was about to break his heart, but nothing could stop him. Not this time.

She didn't seem to hear him come up behind her and started at the touch of his fingertips on her shoulder. As she turned, he pulled her in, holding her tightly to him. She felt stiff at first, almost breakable. Then with a moan, she softened in his arms, leaning into him, her arms coming around him, holding on as if against a fierce, cold wind.

They stood like that for a long time, neither speaking. Grayson waited until he felt some of her strength return. Then, taking her shoulders in his hands, he stepped back to look into her eyes.

"Tell me," he said, his voice a hoarse whisper.

KATE GAZED into her husband's wonderful, open face, tears brimming in her eyes.

"Tell me," he repeated, his hands cupping her shoulders and tightening slightly, his gaze holding hers captive.

She swallowed, afraid yet unable to keep this from him any longer.

"It's just you and me," he said.

She nodded and bit her lip at the compassion she saw in his expression. "Could we sit down?"

He led her over to the couch and sat next to her, holding her hands in his.

She took a deep breath and let it out. "I…I had a baby." The words tumbled out, falling over each other. "It was the year Dad died. I was so alone, so scared, still mourning my father's death and the loss of the ranch. I felt like everything I'd loved was gone."

"What about the father of the baby?" he asked quietly.

"He was otherwise engaged," she said, guilt-ridden for what she'd done to all of their lives. "I was so selfish, Grayson, so stupid."

"No, Kate," he said, emotion making his voice tight as he pulled her to him. "You were young and obviously needed someone. Honey, I'm so sorry."

She was crying now, needing to let it all out. "The baby's father…"

Grayson pulled back to look at her, his eyes widened a little as if he knew what she was going to say.

"He still lives around here," she said, and felt him tense. "I hated him for not standing by me when I needed him. Hated him and loved him."

"Have you seen him since you've been back?"

She nodded.

"Are you still in love with him?"

She heard how hard the words were for Grayson to say. "No." She'd said it too quickly. "I don't know how I feel about him," she said truthfully. "But I do know how I feel about you. *I love you.* This isn't about him."

Grayson studied her openly. "What *is* it about, Kate?"

"The baby I gave up twenty-six years ago. I have to find her."

Chapter Ten

Once outside the cabin, Jerilyn ran to the car, anxious to get away and fearful the cowboy could come busting out of the house at any time.

She had the gun, but she'd also seen the look in that man's eyes. She wasn't sure the .22 would stop him before he took it away from her.

Sliding behind the steering wheel, Jerilyn inserted the key into the ignition as Maddie opened the passenger-side door and awkwardly climbed in with the hedge trimmers gripped in both her hands.

"You all right?" Jerilyn asked, noticing that Maddie seemed a little dazed.

But she nodded and slammed the door as Jerilyn started the engine and threw the car into Reverse.

"Who are you?"

Jerilyn shot her a look as she backed the car up and bumped into a small pine tree. "My name's Jerilyn Larch." She shifted into first gear and glanced toward the cabin. She imagined the cowboy had heard the car engine, raced into the living room and discovered that Maddie was gone.

"Jerilyn Larch?" Maddie repeated blankly as if trying to place the name.

As she hit the gas, Jerilyn saw the cowboy come flying out the front door.

"The door locks don't work," Maddie said, her voice high as the man lunged for the car, grabbing the handle on the passenger-side door.

Jerilyn watched her daughter grip the hedge trimmers in her hands, ready to run them through the man if he managed to get the door open.

But the car was moving too fast. He couldn't get his footing. Still he held on, letting the car drag him along the bumpy road. Jerilyn knew how to put an end to this. She cut the wheel toward a stand of ponderosa pines along the edge of the narrow lane.

There was a loud thud and a cry as the man was nailed by one tree and then another.

When Jerilyn looked in the rearview mirror, she saw him lying unmoving on the side of the road and looking like nothing more than a bundle of dirty clothing. Served him right.

"Who was that man?" she asked.

"Bo Evans." Maddie's voice sounded hoarse as she glanced over her shoulder to where the man lay beside the road.

Jerilyn had seen the bruises on her neck. "Your boyfriend?"

"Former. A low point in my life."

Jerilyn nodded. "I hear ya." She thought about Earl Ray and realized he was no better than this Bo Evans. "I thought I saw a jacket behind the seat."

Maddie reached back to get it. Jerilyn watched her glance again to where Bo lay in a crumpled heap and then quickly turn to the front as she pulled the jacket on and zipped it up, covering her nakedness.

Jerilyn sped up, wondering what she was going to do now that she had her daughter.

MADDIE DIDN'T WANT to think about Bo Evans as she looked over at the woman behind the wheel. As a precaution she leaned the hedge trimmers against the seat within easy reach.

She realized that Jerilyn had been in the restaurant just before closing. She'd eaten alone at the table by the window. She'd also left a very large tip. Too large a tip.

Maddie remembered that she had felt the woman watching her. Jerilyn had given her the creeps just as she did now, even though Maddie knew she should be grateful. The woman had saved her from Bo.

"How did you find me?" Maddie asked.

The blonde glanced over at her for a moment. "I saw him grab you outside the restaurant. There wasn't anyone around to help, so I followed the car."

The explanation seemed plausible enough. So why didn't she feel safe?

Her uneasy feeling amped up when Jerilyn turned south instead of heading back toward town.

"Whitehorse is back the other way," Maddie said, reminding herself that the woman had said earlier that she wasn't from around here. She didn't know the area.

"I have to get my pickup. It's just up the road. It was faster to take his car and make sure he couldn't use it to come after us," Jerilyn said. "Not that he's going anywhere ever again."

Maddie thought of the body she'd seen beside the road. Was Bo really dead? She tried to feel something but came up empty.

Everything about this felt all wrong, she thought, as she looked at the woman behind the wheel, a woman she'd never seen before tonight. Why would a complete stranger risk her life to save her?

And what woman just happened to carry around a .22 pistol?

"Relax," Jerilyn said, smiling over at her as if she could feel Maddie's growing anxiety. "I'm a friend."

She had her doubts about that.

"So what did you do to tick off this Bo Evans?" Jerilyn asked as she drove.

Maddie bristled. "Nothing. He was born that way. I just made the mistake of thinking for a while that I deserved being mistreated." She realized that was probably the most honest she'd ever been about her time with Bo.

"I know just what you mean. My ex, Earl Ray, he could be such a bastard. But then he'd be real sweet, you know?"

Maddie knew. Like some of the women Maddie had met in her support group, Jerilyn had the look of an abused woman. The dullness in the eyes. The lines on her face were a sign of a lot of hard miles. The gravelly whiskey voice. This woman had spent some quality time down on her luck.

She watched Jerilyn glance in the rearview mirror as if afraid they were being followed.

"You have any idea who he called back there?" Jerilyn asked.

Maddie had forgotten about the call Bo had made. She'd been too busy trying to get away. "I wasn't paying any attention."

"I heard him say something like, 'You can have her in the morning.' Have any idea what that might have been about?"

"No." Bo couldn't have been talking about her, could he?

Jerilyn shot her a worried look. "Is there anyone who might pay to get their hands on you?"

"Why would you even ask me that?"

"Because I heard your old boyfriend say something about negotiating more money for you."

Maddie stared at the woman. Her head ached from being banged around by Bo and exhaustion dragged at her. She just wanted to go home, get a hot bath, go to bed and put all of this behind her.

Jerilyn slowed the car and turned into the pines. For a minute, Maddie didn't see the older pickup parked off the road. It was the same year as her own and almost the same color. Jerilyn parked next to the truck and shut off the lights and engine.

"We'll take my pickup from here." She glanced over at Maddie. "That your purse on the floor? Grab it and come on."

Maddie gripped the hedge trimmers and didn't move. The plates on the pickup were local, but Jerilyn had said she was from Arizona. So whose truck was it?

"Why don't you drive?" Jerilyn asked as she handed her the keys.

Maddie didn't take them. Every instinct told her not to get into that pickup with this woman.

Jerilyn reached into her pocket and pulled out the .22, leveling it at Maddie's head. "I need you to do what I say, okay? The last thing I want to do is hurt you."

"I don't understand. What is it you want from me?" Maddie asked, hearing the tears on the edge of her words. She'd been through so much tonight, and now this?

"We need to talk," Jerilyn said. "That's all. Then I'll get you home safe and sound. Let's just go someplace where we don't have to worry about anyone bothering us."

Who would bother them? "Talk about what?"

The blonde only smiled and motioned with the gun for Maddie to take the keys and purse and get out of the car.

SHANE DROVE the two-lane highway through rolling grasslands silvered by the moonlight. The land stretched to the far reaches of the horizon, unbroken except for the black etched outline of the Little Rockies off to the west.

His headlights picked up several sets of eyes ahead. He slowed and saw a half-dozen deer grazing in the barrow pit. One of the deer bolted across the road, bounding through the path of the pickup's headlights, just inches in front of his grill.

Once past the deer, Shane sped up again, feeling the

night slipping away and his fears for Maddie growing with each tick of the clock. Over the next hill, he spotted a large herd of antelope, their hides gleaming white and gold in the moonlight. The animals looked as if they should have been in Africa not Montana.

He hadn't seen another car since he left Whitehorse, which wasn't that surprising for the time of the night and where he was: No Man's Land. Right now he felt the full weight of this isolated country. There hadn't been any ranch lights for miles. No sense of another human. He could see why this part of the state was said to be the loneliest on earth.

As he neared the Missouri Breaks, the land rose in rough limestone buttes and dipped into thousands of juniper– and scrub-pine–filled coulees. Ponderosa pines stood along the buttes, etched black against the night sky.

"There's other ways to get there," Cody had said. "Lots of back roads, passable as long as they're dry, but this would be the fastest way to get to the cabin."

Shane felt the land dropping toward the river. Pine trees popped up in his headlights like sentinels and bluffs rose up, glowing in the moonlight. He felt as though he were on another planet as he dipped down into the rugged Breaks, all the time thinking that the Barneses' cabin couldn't be in a more isolated place.

MADDIE STARED at the gun in the woman's hand, then climbed out of the car. Jerilyn slid out right after her, and they walked over to the pickup.

"Why can't we talk here?" Maddie asked.

Jerilyn shook her head, and with the pistol trained

on her, climbed into the driver's side, pulling Maddie after her.

"You do know how to drive a stick shift, don't you?" Jerilyn asked, when Maddie had settled behind the wheel. "After all, you are a Montana girl, although you should have been an Arizona girl."

Maddie started the engine, her head swimming.

"Go back up the road we came on until you see the turnoff that will take us down to that fishing access."

Maddie hesitated until she felt the barrel of the .22 dig into her side. The road to the river would only take them deeper into the Breaks and farther from help.

"You would have liked growing up in Arizona."

"I don't think so."

Her answer seemed to upset Jerilyn. "You would have been happy in Arizona. I would have seen that you were happy."

Maddie's alarm shot up to a whole new level at the absurdity of this argument—and the fact that Jerilyn was now crying.

Maddie had suspected the woman wasn't stable. No normal woman would have followed Bo's car into the Breaks after seeing her waitress abducted.

"I would have been a good mother to you," Jerilyn said through her tears. "I really would have."

"I'm sure you would have," Maddie said, trying to calm the woman. "But I had a mother."

"That woman wasn't your mother," Jerilyn cried. *"I was!"*

As Maddie drove down the road deeper into the Breaks, she thought she'd misheard the woman.

"I'm *your mother, your* real *mother, your* birth *mother.*"

She shot Jerilyn a look.

"Didn't you notice the resemblance?"

"There are a lot of women with our same coloring," Maddie said, and then wished she'd bitten her tongue.

"I knew you were my daughter the minute I saw you at the restaurant." She sounded proud of that. "I figured your adoptive parents wouldn't tell you. I asked the orderly about them. Your mother couldn't have babies so she took mine. I was only sixteen, just a baby myself, but I could have raised you if my mama had let me."

Maddie tried to concentrate on her driving as the road got more rough and narrow. Of course Sarah Cavanaugh had given birth to her. There was no reason to doubt that, not after hearing her whole life how terrible the birth had been and how much she owed her mother.

"The orderly who told me about your mother got their names and yours for me," Jerilyn was saying. "Roy and Sarah Cavanaugh. That's how I found out that they'd named you Madeline but called you Maddie."

Maddie almost drove off the road.

"See, I really am your mother," Jerilyn was saying. "I've always wanted to come see you, but my mama was sure I would screw up your life like I had mine."

No, this couldn't be true. "If you really were my mother, you wouldn't be pointing a gun at me."

Jerilyn laughed. "It's the only way I can get you to listen to what I have to tell you."

"That's not true."

Jerilyn's face twisted into one of anger. "Why are

you driving so slow?" she demanded. "Speed up or we'll never get far enough away."

"Away from what?"

"Just drive. I know you probably won't believe this, but I came from a family with a good name, lots of money, property and status. It's not my fault that things changed, and that now I need my daughter's help."

Maddie shot her another look. "I don't have any money if that's what you're after."

"But your cousins do. I saw that fancy restaurant. At those prices, your cousin must do just fine."

"You're kidnapping me?"

EARL RAY COULDN'T HELP being excited. He'd have the little black notebook back soon. He thought about the first thing he'd buy himself with all that money. A ticket out of the country, if he was smart.

He didn't like to think about the people he'd taken the book from or what they would do if they found out he had it.

Instead, he thought about Jerilyn and the look on her face when he showed up with her precious daughter. Talk about priceless.

When he'd gone by Buck Jones's house, he'd found his damned stolen car in the drive, but no sign of Jerilyn—or Buck. One of the neighbors had confirmed what Earl Ray had suspected.

Jerilyn had left alone in Buck's truck.

Jerilyn was looking for Maddie, and now Bo Evans swore he had her. Earl Ray thought he might be seeing Jerilyn sooner than he first thought.

As they drove south, he tracked the location of the cell phone he'd given Bo. He felt anxious.

He'd miss Jerilyn, but he couldn't see her in his life anymore. In fact, if she'd found the little black book, he couldn't see her in anyone's life anymore, including her own. He couldn't have her loud mouth telling everyone about the book, and who'd stolen it.

The woman wasn't completely stupid. If she'd found the book, she would know it was worth something. He hated to think she might try to make her own deal for it.

"Not on your life," Earl Ray said under his breath.

"You say somethin'?" Dude asked from behind the wheel.

"We're getting close to where we have to turn. You'd better slow down."

As Dude turned onto an even narrower dirt road, Earl Ray checked his gun, anxious to give Bo Evans what he had coming to him.

MADDIE HAD TO DO something. They were driving deeper into the Breaks, farther and farther away from the chance of finding help and escaping this dangerous woman.

As the pickup topped a small rise in the road, Maddie saw the moon reflected in a small pond up ahead just off the right side of the road. When she'd gotten into the pickup, she'd buckled her seat belt and deactivated the passenger-side air bag after noticing Jerilyn hadn't buckled up. Jerilyn sat sideways on the seat, the .22 pistol trained on her.

As Maddie dropped down the hill, she told herself what she was planning was risky, but staying in this pickup with this crazy woman could be more dangerous.

The pond didn't look very deep, but Maddie put down her window just in case.

"What's wrong with you? It's freezing out there," Jerilyn complained.

"I just need a little air."

"Put that window up! What's that?"

The pickup started swerving back and forth in the ruts. "I think we have a flat tire!"

"Stop the truck!"

"I'm trying."

"Hit the brakes!" Jerilyn yelled, taking the pistol off her as she swung around to look at the road ahead. "Look out!"

Maddie had swerved and braked a little pretending they had a flat. As they came down the hill, she swerved and headed straight for the pond.

The pickup bounced over the uneven earth beside the road and hit the water, the front end breaking the moon-slick surface and sending up a spray over the windshield and in through Maddie's open window. The front of the truck plowed through the water for a dozen yards before finally coming to a stop, the tires sinking into the mud.

Out of the corner of her eye, she saw Jerilyn hit the windshield with a thud. Maddie knew she had to move fast. Even before the truck came to a full stop, she unsnapped her seat belt and reached for the door handle.

Chapter Eleven

Grayson held Kate until she fell back to sleep. Then, unable to sleep, he got up and wandered through the empty house. Shane's truck wasn't in front of his cabin. That in itself was odd. But Shane was a grown man. If he decided to stay out all night that was fine. Juanita lived in one of the guesthouses some distance from the ranch house. He'd wanted them all to have plenty of room. He'd wanted Trails West to be a haven for them all.

Out on the porch, Grayson dropped into a chair and looked across the moonlight-drenched land. He feared his plan to get his sons to Montana wasn't going to work, no matter how much he yearned for it. All this space, all these added cabins he'd had built for family and company, and yet he and Kate were probably going to end up here alone.

He'd told himself that he'd bought this place for Kate. But a part of him had hoped to find a little of his Rebecca still here. Sometimes he thought he could hear her laughter on the breeze or look up and see her riding across the prairie toward him. He knew how much she'd loved living here, riding her horse over these rolling plains.

He had a photograph of her astride a pretty paint horse at the age of eleven, all pigtails and grin.

Even with the memories of Rebecca so strong here, the move had only strengthened his love for Kate. She was his connection to the past and the present—the bridge that had helped him heal. Their love for each other was what he'd hoped would bring the family together. His family.

Now to find out that Kate had a twenty-six-year-old daughter… A daughter she gave up. A daughter she had with a man who still lived in Whitehorse.

Grayson hated that the news had kicked his feet out from under him. He'd known Kate had had lovers. But this mystery lover shared a child with her. That was something Grayson could never do with her, and he found himself unable to hold back the surge of jealousy he felt toward the man.

He didn't turn as he heard the front door open and Kate pad across the porch to him. He didn't want her to see him like this. Hell, right now he could barely stand himself. He thought he was a better man.

But the moment she touched his arm, he felt that eternal connection between them. This was his Kate. She loved him. And God knew he loved her.

She curled up on his lap, and he held her to him.

"I'm so sorry," she whispered. "I should have told you long before now."

"It's why you never came back here, isn't it?" he asked after a moment.

She nodded.

So he'd opened this can of worms by buying the ranch and not even thinking to discuss it with her. He chuckled at his own foolishness.

"Can you ever forgive me?" she asked softly, as the breeze teased at her hair.

"There is nothing to forgive." He drew back, so he could see her face in the moonlight. "We'll find your daughter. No matter what it takes, if that's what you want."

Tears welled in her eyes, and she bent to cover his mouth with her own. He deepened the kiss as he rose. Grayson renewed his resolve that this ranch would one day ring with the voices and laughter of their family, and carried his wife back into the house.

EVEN THOUGH there was only a little water against it, it took all of Maddie's strength to push open the pickup door.

As she slipped out, she glanced back at Jerilyn, who lay crumpled on the floorboard breathing but not moving. No sign of the gun.

Maddie dropped into the pond. The cold water took her breath away, even though it was only waist deep.

She sank in the mud and had to struggle to take a step. Behind her Jerilyn called out her name.

"Maddie?"

She heard Jerilyn and tried to hurry. The moon shone down, making her a perfect target.

Jerilyn couldn't be her mother. No mother would threaten to shoot her daughter. Maddie felt a chill at both the thought and the cold pond water. Sarah Cavanaugh had been a terrible mother. But Jerilyn? If Maddie had been adopted, she would have known, wouldn't she?

She shuddered as she recalled how cold and distant Sarah had been. Nothing like a real mother. But Maddie had Geraldine next door, and Sarah hadn't seemed to mind that she found love and affection at the older woman's house instead of her own.

"Maddie! Come back here! You have to help me!"

Maddie was almost to the shore. She could hear Jerilyn still banging around in the cab of the pickup as if looking for something. The gun?

"You did that on purpose!" Jerilyn was yelling. "You drove into this damned pond. You little beast. You could have killed us both!"

Maddie heard Jerilyn open the passenger-side door and splash down into the water. Something metallic banged against the side of the truck. She had apparently found the gun. As Jerilyn worked her way along the side of the truck, Maddie could hear the steady tap of the gun in her hand.

She tried to hurry, thankful the pickup was between her and Jerilyn, but with each step, the mud sucked down her boots and the snowmelt pond water lapped up, freezing cold.

"Don't leave me," Jerilyn screamed after her. *"You have to help me. I'm your mother!"* The woman sounded close to hysterical.

Maddie didn't look back as she reached the shore. Across the narrow dirt road, the pines were thick, the land dropping off toward Old Town Whitehorse. Country Maddie knew.

She ran toward the road, knowing that for a few moments she would be silhouetted against the moonlight and provide a clear target if Jerilyn was serious about shooting her.

"Maddie!"

A bullet whizzed past her ear as she raced across the road and headed for the shelter of the pines. She reached the trees as the sound of another .22 gunshot filled the air. Maddie dove deeper into the pines, afraid Jerilyn was chasing her.

She caught her foot on a tree root and fell headfirst, skidding across the long-dried ponderosa pine needles to crash into the trunk of a pine.

Her shoulder was on fire from hitting the tree. Dragging herself up into a sitting position under the tree boughs, she took a few moments to let the pain subside and catch her breath. From the shadows of the big pine tree, she could see the road and the crazy woman standing in the middle of it.

Jerilyn was squinting into the pines. She didn't seem to be wearing shoes. Earlier she'd been wearing some low-heeled pumps. They were no doubt stuck in the mud of the pond.

Maddie didn't dare move, fearing Jerilyn would see her the moment she stepped out in the moonlight. The ponderosa boughs formed a protective shelter from the light, the ground under them dark and soft with dried needles.

Holding her breath, she tried to move her shoulder. It didn't feel broken. The skin on her hands burned from where she'd scraped them when she fell, and she had a stitch in her side from slogging out of the pond and running into the trees.

She leaned back against the tree trunk, prepared to run again if Jerilyn made a move toward her.

But Maddie told herself that the woman couldn't see her, and that as long as she stayed where she was, hidden under this pine, she was safe. She prayed that was true as she tried to catch her breath, her terror making her side ache with each gasp. She was hurt, weak and exhausted and felt frighteningly fragile, afraid she couldn't take much more before she broke.

As her breathing slowed, she heard the growl of a car engine coming up the road. Suddenly the glow of headlights washed over the pines.

Maddie shrank back as she saw Jerilyn move to the edge of the road and hide the .22 behind her back.

Maddie wanted to scream. Someone who could help her was coming up the road. People in this part of the state wouldn't hesitate to stop the moment they saw a pickup in the pond. But the person wouldn't know Jerilyn was crazy—or that she was armed and dangerous.

The car slowed as it approached, the taillights flashing red. Maddie couldn't let an innocent, well-meaning person get killed because of her. She pushed herself away from the trunk of the pine, and on hands and knees she began to crawl out into the moonlight.

EARL RAY HAD NEVER BEEN so glad to see anyone. Here was Jerilyn standing beside the road looking like a drowned rat.

He didn't even have to ask what had happened, given that the pickup was partially submerged in the pond beside the road, the driver-side door hanging open.

He lowered his window. "Kind of hard on other people's cars, aren't you?"

"Earl Ray." She said his name as if she'd just seen him a few minutes before—as if she hadn't stolen his car and money, left him in a fleabag motel in the desert and forced him to come a thousand miles to find her sorry behind.

"What the hell is wrong with you, woman?" he demanded, losing his temper as she bent down to look in his open window.

"Not a damned thing you can't fix," she said with a smile. "Aren't you glad to see me, Earl Ray?"

"Where's my notebook? I know you found it."

"I did," she said, nodding, a change coming over her eyes. "Is that all you care about, your stupid notebook?"

"Where is it, Jerilyn?" He grabbed hold of a fistful of her mud-covered blouse.

"I threw it out the window of the car on my way to Montana."

He only had an instant to shove her back and duck as she thrust a .22 pistol through the window.

The shot echoed through the rented SUV but did nothing to blot out Dude's shriek of pain. She kept firing blindly. Earl Ray heard Bubba let out a curse and slump heavily against the backseat.

Earl Ray threw open his door as Jerilyn took off across the road toward the pond, her last shot going wild. He clambered out after her, not sure he hadn't been hit until he was on his feet. At the edge of the road, Jerilyn turned as if to fire back at him.

But he was right behind her.

"You're a lousy bastard, Earl Ray Pitts. I hope you rot in hell."

He tackled her, his momentum driving them off the road and into the soft mud at the edge of the pond. He fell on top of her, Jerilyn still screaming obscenities. The sound of the gunshot came as a complete surprise.

Hot liquid splattered across his face, and he swore, certain this time she'd hit him. His hands went for her throat. The crazy broad wasn't going to shoot him again.

Everything had gone quiet. Dude had even stopped shrieking. Earl Ray doubted that was a good sign.

He tightened his fingers around Jerilyn's scrawny throat, not realizing why it was suddenly so quiet until he looked at her face. Her cheek was caked with mud, and her eyes were more vacant than usual.

It took him a moment to understand what had happened. When he'd tackled her, driving her down into the soft mud, the .22 had been between them and she'd fired. His weight had flattened the gun between their bodies, forcing the barrel to be pointed right at Jerilyn's throat. A straight shot to her brain.

"Oh hell." He jerked his hands from her neck and stared down at his warm, bloodstained fingers.

Scrambling to his feet, he told himself he hadn't meant to kill her. He'd planned to let Dude or Bubba do it—after he got his notebook. Now everything was screwed.

He staggered back, wiping the blood on his pants and

trying to calm down. He swore as he wiped his sleeve over his face and realized he was sweating. *Jerilyn was dead.*

Earl Ray glanced up the road, thankful it was still the middle of the night. All he needed was some rancher to come along. As far as they were from civilization, he doubted the road got much use, but he couldn't chance it.

"Dude!" he called to the SUV. "Bubba!" Neither answered. He looked at the pickup out in the pond. He was going to have to go out there himself. She could have been lying about the notebook, he told himself. It could still be in her purse.

The water was freezing and the glue-like mud took one of his shoes with the first step. He retrieved it, stepped back to the shore and took off the other shoe before wading out again.

Both of the pickup's doors were open. He worked his way out to the driver's side and peered in.

The purse on the seat wasn't the one Jerilyn had in Arizona. When had she had time to buy a new one? He dug through the contents, using the dome light. No little black book.

He let out a curse. This wasn't Jerilyn's purse. Squinting at the driver's license, he saw that it belonged to Madeline Cavanaugh. Maddie Cavanaugh?

The hair stood up on the back of his neck. He'd been so upset it hadn't registered that both doors of the pickup had been open. That's because there'd been a passenger. That's why Maddie's purse was in this pickup with Jerilyn?

He let out another curse and quickly searched the rest of the pickup. Jerilyn's purse was on the floorboard, down in the murky water. He rummaged through it, hoping he could save the book and the writing inside.

But his little black book wasn't in her purse.

"She wouldn't have thrown it out," he said to himself. She wasn't that dumb. Or was she?

He felt along the floorboard, thinking maybe the book had fallen out. All he found was a pair of hedge trimmers. He didn't even want to think about what they were for as he backed out of the pickup's cab and started toward shore.

A thought struck him. What if Jerilyn had shown Maddie his black book and told her to keep it if anything ever happened to her?

He tore off his muddy socks and pulled on his shoes. Climbing back up to the road, he looked toward the woods and saw what he knew would be there. Footprints in the soft earth at the edge of the road and tracks heading into the woods.

Maddie Cavanaugh was out there somewhere. He could almost feel her presence, and there was little doubt in his mind that she would have heard the gunshots and the screams. She was a potential witness to murder.

But he was more worried about what Jerilyn might have given her for safekeeping.

MADDIE HAD BEEN PARTWAY out of the trees when she'd heard Jerilyn call by name the man who'd pulled over— Earl Ray. She'd said her boyfriend's name was Earl Ray. That had barely sunk in when she'd heard the shots and the shrieks and Jerilyn screaming. She'd ducked back under the pine, afraid that they would see her if she ran.

Now she huddled under the dark boughs, praying that Earl Ray and whoever else had stopped for Jerilyn would just drive off.

Then a twig snapped, and a large dark shape appeared at the edge of the pines.

Her heart lodged in her throat as he called her name.

"Maddie? I know you're out there. Why don't you come on out? I won't hurt you. I'm a friend of your mother's."

A shudder quaked through her. He knew she was out here. Knew her name. Thought Jerilyn was her mother. But she didn't believe for a moment he was a friend.

Maddie held her breath, forcing herself not to move. Where was Jerilyn? What about the other sounds she'd heard? Her every instinct told her that Jerilyn was dead. So were the others, the ones this man had called Dude and Bubba.

She could see the man but was sure that he couldn't see her.

A cell phone rang, the sound coming from his car. He ignored it. "Come on, Maddie. I'll give you a ride back to town. You've had a rough night. I know you're anxious to see your family."

The cell phone rang again. He let out a curse and turned back toward the road.

She waited until he reached the SUV before she leapt to her feet and ran. Her heart was pounding too hard to hear if he came after her.

OVER THE SOUND of his ringing cell phone, Earl Ray thought he'd heard something move in the woods. But when he'd swung around and looked, he saw nothing but moonlight and shadows in the trees.

He found the cell phone where he'd dropped it. Only one person had this number.

"What the hell do you want?" he snapped.

"I'm hurt," Bo said. "I need you to come get me and take me to a doctor."

Earl Ray laughed. "But I don't know where you are. Too bad you didn't give me Maddie tonight like I asked you to," he said through gritted teeth. "You still have her, right?"

Silence. "I did. But someone took her," Bo finally admitted.

Earl Ray walked around the SUV. His first thought was to leave Bo wherever he was and let the bastard die. But as desperate as the kid sounded, he'd probably do something stupid like call for an ambulance.

Cursing under his breath, Earl Ray opened the driver-side door. Dude was sitting behind the wheel, blood pooled in his lap. Bubba didn't look much better in the backseat.

With distaste, Earl Ray leaned over Dude, unbuckled his seatbelt and pulled with his free hand. Dude tumbled out on the road. Once out of the car, Dude was fairly easy to kick off into the barrow pit. Bubba, he pulled out and rolled down the slope into the trees.

"Tell me where I can find you," Earl Ray said to Bo. He listened with little interest, since he was already close by and just needed the last detailed directions to find Bo.

According to what Bo told him, the cabin was just down the road.

"Are you alone?" Earl Ray asked.

"Yes. Don't worry. I'll find Maddie for you. I swear. Just get me medical attention first."

"Yeah, sure. I'll be right there." Earl Ray disconnected as he spotted a set of headlights in the distance headed up the road.

THE SKY TO THE EAST opened a crack at the first sign of daylight. Shane noticed the shimmering orange glow along the horizon but it was still dark here in the mountains. Ahead the land dropped toward the Missouri River, the pine trees taller and thicker on each side of the road.

A few miles down the road, his headlights picked up the shine of chrome just off the road. Shane slowed, his pulse rate jumping up at the sight of the pickup in the middle of the small pond off the side of the road.

"Buck Jones's pickup." Shane swore under his breath as he brought his truck to a stop, grabbed his flashlight and jumped out. Both truck doors were hanging open, and even from the road he could see that the cab was empty. No sign of Jerilyn or Maddie.

As he looked down for footprints in the soft earth around the pond, Shane spotted a body half-buried in the mud at the edge of the water. For one heart-stopping moment, all he saw was the mud-caked blond hair. Maddie.

He shone the flashlight beam in the woman's face. It was Jerilyn. She matched the description Buck had given him.

The beam shone on the gunshot wound under her chin. Shane felt an icy cold fear brush the back of his neck as he examined the ground around the body.

Footprints. Too large to be Maddie's. Was it possible Maddie hadn't been with Jerilyn? That the woman had picked up a man?

As he directed his flashlight beam along the edge of the road he found two other bodies, both too large to be Maddie. Shane searched the ground for more tracks and finally found smaller boot prints coming out of the pond. He followed them across the road, where the tracks were much farther apart. The woman had been running.

Unfortunately, the boot tracks ended in the fallen pine needles of the forest.

He flashed the light out over the ponderosa pines.

"Maddie?" He called again, louder. "It's Shane. Shane Corbett."

No answer.

As he walked over to the bodies, he recognized one of the men as the same one he'd seen talking to Bo Evans the night of the rodeo dance.

Climbing back into his truck, Shane used his cell to call the sheriff's office and report what he'd found. He'd hoped when he called that the dispatcher would tell him that Maddie had been found, alive and safe, but he'd known better the moment he'd seen the tracks going into the woods and not coming out again.

The dispatcher told him to stay at the scene until the sheriff got there. A search-and-rescue helicopter would be called in to help search once dawn broke.

Shane couldn't just sit there and wait. Not when his every instinct told him that Maddie was out there some-where—most likely along with two very dangerous men.

EARL RAY TURNED at the tree with the Barnes sign tacked on it and followed the directions Bo had given him. After he'd seen another vehicle headed this way, he needed to get Bo and find Maddie and the notebook as quickly as possible.

As he drove toward the cabin, he noticed a piece of clothing stuck to the bark of a tree along the edge of the road. The cloth looked soaked with blood. He slowed. There were tracks, as if something had been dragged. Several twigs were snapped off the trees and there was a scrape on one of the pines where the bark had been rubbed off. It all looked fresh—including what appeared to be droplets of blood in the dust.

There were more scuff marks in front of the cabin. And more blood. What the hell had gone on here tonight?

Earl Ray could only imagine, given who was involved. But he had to wonder how Bo had apparently gotten the worst of it.

He drew his gun. It was no little peashooter like the one Jerilyn had used to kill Dude and Bubba and herself. This was a man's gun for a man's job. Earl Ray didn't bother to shut off the engine as he got out.

An owl hooted, making him tense as he neared the

cabin entrance. The door was ajar, a smear of blood on the steps, and from inside came the sound of moaning.

"Bo?" Earl Ray called.

"In here."

Earl Ray smiled as he stepped inside. "Ready for that ride I promised you?"

MADDIE DIDN'T KNOW how far she'd run. Time had lost all meaning to her. She ran because that was all she could do, sprinting down the mountainside through the trees, pale light flickering in the boughs as the day began to dawn. Even when she felt the hitch in her side again, even when she thought she couldn't run another step, she kept going.

She thought she knew where she was, that the occasional rock butte or tall pine looked familiar. She had headed in the direction of the Breaks to the south of Old Town Whitehorse. As a girl, she'd ridden her horse all through this country and knew a place where she would be safe.

She ran as if the killer were right behind her. But she knew she was also running from what Jerilyn had told her. She didn't look back, not since she'd scrambled from the shelter of the pine. She feared falling—or worse, seeing Earl Ray Pitts right behind her.

For all she knew, he was practically breathing down her neck. With each running stride, she expected to hear him or feel the burning fire of a bullet as it slammed into her back.

She ran blind through the pines, tears streaming down her face, everything a blur. Over the sound of her ragged breathing and the thunder of her pulse, she didn't hear the vehicle, didn't see the headlights or even realize she had reached a road until the lights flashed over her, catching her like a deer in their glare.

Maddie stumbled and fell, sprawling across the dirt road directly in front of the vehicle.

Chapter Twelve

The sun glowed behind the pines to the east, blindingly bright as it spread across the country, highlighting the rocky bluffs and making the ponderosa pines shimmer.

Shane caught the movement out of the corner of his eye only a heartbeat before the person came running out of the woods and onto the road in front of his truck.

In that instant, he saw the head of blond hair. Saw the woman look up in surprise. Saw the look of sheer terror in her blue eyes. *Maddie*.

Shane slammed on his brakes and turned the wheel hard to the left. The pickup left the road, skidding off and down the incline into the pines.

The tree came up fast. The front of the pickup crashed into the thick trunk, the heavy boughs slamming against the windshield as his air bag exploded in his face.

ALL MADDIE HAD SEEN was the grill of the vehicle coming at her. Earl Ray. When she'd seen the vehicle bearing down on her, all she could think was that this killer had found her.

Maddie scrambled to her feet. As she did, her hand brushed a weathered tree limb lying at the edge of the road. She snatched it up and took off running down the road as she heard a door open.

This time, she heard him behind her. Heard the pounding of his shoes on the hard road. He was gaining on her. In fact, he was right behind her, calling her name just as he had earlier.

She swung around, using the limb like a club. Only at the last minute did it register that she knew this man.

"Maddie!" Shane ducked the limb, lunged at her and took her down at the edge of the road. They tumbled into the soft earth and tall green grass.

She struggled under him for a moment, all her adrenaline still pumping.

"It's okay. *It's me. Maddie, it's Shane.*"

She blinked up into the bright day, finally focusing on his face. It really was Shane Corbett.

"I…I…" Her voice broke, and all the fight went out of her. He rolled off her and brushed back a lock of her hair from her face. She saw his expression and knew what she must look like with her bruised, cut face.

"Who did this to you?" he asked, his voice low, husky and tinged with fury.

She shook her head. What did it matter? His warm hand felt so good against her skin as he gently cupped her jaw, his thumb pad brushing her cheek, his eyes full of compassion. She leaned into his hand and closed her eyes and whispered, "Bo."

She heard Shane curse under his breath. He helped her to her feet, and she saw his pickup, wrecked down in the trees. She shivered, realizing they had no way to drive out of here and that Earl Ray must still be looking for her.

"He's looking for me." She hadn't realized she'd spoken the words out loud until Shane told her not to worry.

"I've called the sheriff. He should be on his way along with a couple of his deputies. They've sent a search-and-rescue chopper, as well."

She nodded but didn't believe everything was going to be all right. Her nerves were on end, and she swore she could hear another vehicle driving along the road. But she'd thought that ever since she'd bolted from her hiding place under the pine. She'd thought she could feel Earl Ray's hot breath on her neck.

She saw Shane reach for something, but he came up empty-handed. "What is it?" she asked, her voice cracking.

"My cell phone. I'm sure it's in the truck. I probably lost it when I hit the tree. Where's Bo now?" Shane asked. He cocked his head, as if he were also listening to something in the distance.

"He's dead." At least he'd looked dead the last time she'd seen him. She gazed into Shane's clear blue eyes and remembered being in his arms on the night of the dance—remembered that fear and excitement. Shane had thought her reactions were because of her fear of Bo.

She no longer had to fear Bo, but that didn't mean this was over. "There's this man," she said. "Earl Ray. He killed this blond woman who said she was my real mother." The words tumbled out. She looked into Shane's handsome face, saw the distress there. "He's after me. He knows I went into the woods. He knows I saw."

Shane nodded and pulled her into his arms again. "The sheriff will find him."

Her limbs trembled. She couldn't remember ever feeling this weak and exhausted or this relieved to see anyone. She leaned into him, feeling his warmth and his strength and wishing she could stay right here forever.

Shane was here to rescue her. That's what the Texas Ranger did. At lunch when he'd tried to warn her about Jud and Bo, he'd wanted to protect her, but she'd been so certain she could take care of herself—that she had no other choice. Now her eyes burned with tears. It took all of her strength not to cry.

Suddenly, the roar of an engine filled the air, and before she could take another breath the front end of an SUV appeared over a rise in the road.

SHANE THOUGHT he'd heard a vehicle coming. It would be the sheriff or one of his deputies. One of them would get Maddie somewhere safe while he and the others made sure Bo Evans was really dead and tracked down Earl Ray Pitts.

The driver had seen them in the road. Shane waited for the vehicle to slow. Instead, he heard the driver give the SUV more gas as it bore down on them.

Shane grabbed Maddie and dove for the ditch. Behind him, all he heard was flying gravel as the driver skidded to a stop.

He and Maddie hit the dirt and rolled. At the edge of

the pines, Shane pulled Maddie to her feet and, taking her hand, ran deeper into the woods.

A car door slammed. An instant later a bullet whizzed through the air next to them. Behind them, Shane heard a twig break. Another bullet zinged past, struck a tree and showered them with bark and dust.

He zigzagged them through the pines, running hard to put as much distance as possible between themselves and the shooter, ignoring the pain in his legs.

Shane knew Maddie had to be exhausted. He'd felt her trembling in his arms back there on the road when he'd first caught up to her, and he'd seen the defeat in her eyes those few seconds before she'd recognized him.

They had a little lead on the shooter, but not much. If they hoped to survive, they had to outrun him. Shane wished he had his gun. But he hadn't touched it since he'd left the hospital. He'd been a fool to leave it in Texas and an even bigger fool not to take one of his father's before he'd left the ranch.

But just the thought of firing a gun again…

He felt her lag behind and saw that she was limping badly. He knew she couldn't go much farther, yet he pulled her along because there was no time for stopping.

"This way," Maddie cried, pulling on his arm as she motioned toward the sheer face of a rock butte off to their right. The sun had caught on the limestone, making it glow golden in the morning light.

As they neared the butte, all Shane could see was a solid wall of rock. "Maddie, we have to keep going," he whispered, as he gasped for breath. He was limping a little, too, a reminder of the last time he'd had to face a criminal with a gun.

"I can't." She was limping too badly now, grimacing with each step. She motioned for him to follow as she made her way to the rock wall.

He went after her, hoping she didn't plan to climb up the face of the cliff. As he neared, Maddie disappeared into a narrow crevice between the rocks. The crack was so well hidden he hadn't seen it.

Shane glanced back the way they'd come. He couldn't see anyone, but he knew they weren't far behind. Maddie had said Bo was dead, but that didn't mean that Earl Ray Pitts was alone.

"Come on," Maddie called, sounding as if she were deep inside the rock.

Hoping she knew what she was doing and that he would fit, he squeezed into the crevice. Because of his size, it was hard to wend his way through the crack. He felt Maddie reach for his hand and guide him in.

To his surprise, the crack opened into a hollow not yet touched by the sun. The space was small, the rock floor filled with several deep, tiny pools that held rainwater. Maddie bent down to cup the clear water and bring it to her lips. He knelt down beside her and did the same.

From what he could tell, they had reached a dead end. The only way out of there was back the way they'd come.

"Maddie, we can't stay here," he whispered. "If they find us, it will be like shooting fish in a barrel."

She gave him a tired smile and touched her fingers to her lips as she got to her feet with a grimace and limped over to another crack in the rocks, this one making a V as it soared upward. She motioned him to follow and began to climb, using the crack for leverage. He could see that she was using the last of her strength and feared the hurt ankle wouldn't hold. One thing was clear. She wouldn't be able to make another run for her life.

"Maddie?"

She disappeared from view again, but he could hear her still climbing. He grasped hold of the rocks and climbed after her.

MADDIE CLIMBED into the cave entrance and stumbled to her knees, her ankle killing her. She couldn't go another step. Tears sprung to her eyes as she crawled over to a corner and rested her back against the cool rock wall.

Shane climbed up through the hole, his eyes widening as he took in the room in the rocks. A shaft of sunlight poured down through a man-sized hole like a chimney above them. He could see blue sky.

"The whole area is a honeycomb of caves," she said. "I found this one quite by accident. I'd seen the opening from the top of the butte and knew there had to be another way to get into here."

"Who knows about this place?" Shane asked, looking worried.

"I never told anyone about it," she said. It was her secret place. She'd never brought anyone here before. Strange, but it seemed right that she was sharing it for the first time with Shane Corbett.

He sat down, leaning against the wall across from

her. Sunlight spilled at their feet, making the room glow with warmth and light. "Nice digs."

She barely had enough energy to return his smile, but when she looked into his eyes she felt a shiver of desire—much as she had the night of the rodeo dance when he'd held her.

Like now, Shane took her reaction for something it wasn't. He'd thought when she'd trembled in his arms at the dance it was from fear of Bo.

Now he thought she was cold. He removed his jacket and reached across the small space to wrap his body-warmed cloth around her. They were so close she could feel his breath on her cheek—so close it would have been impossible not to kiss him. She'd secretly wanted to for long enough.

Maddie brushed her mouth over his, closing her eyes as she felt an incredible tingle from her lips to the tip of her toes. Chemistry. She'd heard about it, but had only felt it the first time she'd seen Shane—the day he came by to pick up her and her horse.

It had scared her then, just as it did now. The difference was that now she felt she had nothing to lose.

"Maddie?" He drew back to look at her.

She cupped his handsome face in the palms of her hands and breathed in the masculine scent of him, drawn like metal to magnet. "Shhhhh."

She saw something spark in his gaze. Had Shane felt the chemistry the first time he'd seen her that day at her house? He'd been so serious, clearly annoyed at his brother and upset because he'd thought Jud was leading her on.

Clueless, as her cousin-in-law Bridger had said.

She leaned into Shane now and kissed him again, tasting him, teasing his lips open. Desire sparked through her; a bolt of electricity jump-started her heart and made her forget her pain, her exhaustion, everything but Shane Corbett.

Maddie lost herself in the pleasure of his mouth, his tongue, his taste.

When he drew back to look at her again, there was a kind of wonder in his gaze.

She smiled and touched his cheek, a day's stubble rough under her fingertips. Everything about this man stirred a passion in her like nothing she'd ever known.

"I'm not sure I understand what's going on," he said.

"Don't you, Shane?"

"Jud—"

"Jud set you up. Set us up."

"What?"

She chuckled as she ran her fingertips along his solid square jaw to his sensual lips. "Weren't you even a little suspicious when he kept throwing us together?"

He frowned.

"I wasn't sure what he was up to until you told me about the marriage pact and that he'd drawn the shortest straw." She smiled. "And I'll bet he promised a wedding, right?"

"How did you know?"

"What would be the best way to give your father what he wanted without having to get married? Find a woman for one of your brothers. Does that sound anything like the Jud you know and love?"

Shane let out a curse. "I knew he was up to something, but I never dreamed…" He met her gaze. "Apparently you know him better than I do."

"I spotted the kind of cowboy he was the first time I saw him. The only reason I went out with him was that my cousins were worried about me. I'd do anything for them. Even date your brother. I knew I couldn't fall for Jud. He wasn't my type, and I didn't believe for a moment he was interested in me."

"I still can't believe Jud would—"

"Believe it. I should have seen it right away," she said. "When Jud and I went out, he ended up talking about you the entire time, what a great brother you were."

Shane laughed. "The little son of a… He said he'd found the perfect woman."

She cocked a brow at that.

"He was right." Shane leaned toward her again. "You *are* perfect."

Perfect for you, Shane Corbett.

He pulled her close, deepening the kiss. His body felt wonderfully strong and warm, and his touch was tender. "I don't want to hurt you," he said, gently touching her bruised face.

"You won't hurt me," she said. Shane Corbett, the Texas Ranger, a man who saved women in distress. She loved that he was shy, and while she knew he'd had his share of women, he was nothing like Jud.

"Are you sure about this?"

She'd never been more sure about anything in her life. While she'd never tell him, Jud was a pretty good matchmaker.

In answer to Shane's question, she wrapped her arms around his neck and pulled him to her. Their lips touched, and an electrical shot sparked through her. She knew Shane had felt it. She heard him groan. His hands cupped her buttocks as he pulled her onto his lap.

SHANE TRAILED KISSES down Maddie's slim throat. His brother and his plot were completely forgotten as he realized he'd wanted this woman from the first time he'd laid eyes on her.

He unzipped the lightweight jacket she wore to reveal her small, perfect breasts. He felt his desire spiral upward like the shaft of sunlight above them.

"Maddie," he whispered, as his mouth dropped to draw a nipple and suck the tip into a hard nub. She shuddered and drew him closer, her back arching.

Shane didn't remember removing the rest of her clothing or his own. He lost himself in her, rocketed higher and higher by her responses to his touch and his to hers. The feeling that they'd always known each other only grew as they finally came, both in sync, as if this had been written in the stars.

Later, when they lay spent in each other's arms, he couldn't help but think about Jud and his belief in destiny. Lying here with Maddie, Shane thought his brother might be right. This had felt destined since the first time he'd seen Maddie sitting on that porch. A Montana cowgirl.

"This was what you were afraid of, wasn't it?" he whispered against her hair. "The night of the rodeo dance. I thought it was Bo you were frightened of, but it was this."

She nodded against his chest. "I had never felt the emotions you evoked in me. Being in your arms…I wasn't ready for those kinds of feelings."

"But you are now?"

She smiled as she gazed up at him. "Almost getting killed changes a person. When I thought I might die before I ever got the chance to kiss you…"

"Tell me what happened to you," he whispered.

Safe in his arms, she told him about Bo abducting her and taking her to the cabin, and about the blond woman from the restaurant saving her.

"She was crazy. She said she was my real mother, that she'd given me up at birth." Maddie must have sensed something in his silence. She leaned up on one elbow and looked at him. "Don't tell me that I share any genes with that woman. *She kidnapped me. What mother kidnaps her own daughter and holds her at gunpoint?*"

He heard her voice break and knew how hard this was for her. "We don't know for certain that Jerilyn Larch is your mother. We won't know until we can run DNA tests."

"I'm afraid because she looks like me."

"A lot of women have blond hair and blue eyes. Like my mother. Like my stepmother Kate. Like your cousins."

Maddie nodded still worried.

"Bo wasn't the only one who hurt you, was he?" he said and, seeing Maddie's reaction, he knew he'd guessed right. "What made you leave and not come back for so long?"

Maddie took a ragged breath. "I just needed to get away." There was an edge to her voice, a don't-mess-with-me tone that he took for fear.

"Who hurt you?"

"Where do you want me to begin? My former fiancé just tried to… Well, who knows what he planned to do to me. My alleged birth mother just tried to kidnap me for ransom and shot at me. My mother, my possibly adoptive mother, Sarah Cavanaugh…" Maddie looked away.

"What did she do?" he asked quietly.

"Do you really want to hear all this?"

"Yes. I want you to be able to put all this behind you. No more secrets. I think keeping this secret is what puts that haunted look in your eyes." The same haunted look he'd seen recently in Kate's eyes. "Trust me, Maddie?"

She softened in his arms. "I'll bet you made a good Texas Ranger."

He liked to think so, but he'd certainly had his doubts, especially recently. As for Maddie, he suspected Bo Evans had just been a symptom. Bo wasn't the kind of man that a woman like Maddie Cavanaugh would go out with unless something had happened to hurt her, to make her feel unworthy of a good man who would love her.

"You can tell me."

He felt her weaken as she looked into his eyes.

"It's a long story," she said at last, and laid her head back on his chest.

"We have time." The cave was hidden well enough, and they should be able to hear anyone coming. Besides, he believed that the only way to get rid of a ghost was to shed light on it.

"My mother, at least the woman I called my mother, Sarah Cavanaugh, was cold and uncaring." Her voice broke. "I spent most of my childhood at the farm next door. Geraldine Shaw was older and very kind to me. She taught me to sew and cook. I loved being in her house because it was warm and cozy. My house was cold like my mother, a showplace, even though we never had anyone over to see it. Geraldine was killed. That's when it came out about Geraldine's husband, Ollie."

Maddie swallowed. He felt her tense against his chest, and her fingers tightened on his rib cage. "I helped her bury Ollie in the rose garden after she killed him. She hit him with a lamp because he was trying to rape me. He had Alzheimer's and he didn't know what he was doing. Neither of us wanted any of this to come out, so we did what we had to do."

Shane sucked in a pained breath as he pulled her tighter against him. "I'm sorry."

She nodded against his chest. "It gets worse," she said in a whisper. "Nick Giovanni was the new deputy in town at the time. The sheriff was in Florida. Nick discovered that someone had been blackmailing Geraldine, bleeding her dry. The blackmailer knew what had happened. I had no idea, but once I heard, I knew she'd been paying the blackmailer to protect me."

Shane felt his heart lodge in his throat as Maddie pulled back to look into his face.

"The blackmailer was my mother, Sarah Cavanaugh."

"Maddie." He drew her closer, stroking her long hair.

"My own mother—a blackmailer," she said, crying now. "Using something horrible that had happened to her daughter and taking advantage of the nice lady next door just for money. But maybe she wasn't my mother. Maybe my real mother is a kidnapper."

He let her cry it out. When she stopped, she lifted her head to look at him. Her smile was enough to break his heart. Shane Corbett knew at that moment that he would love this woman until the day he died.

They made love again as if the world outside this cavern no longer existed. Wrapped in Shane's arms, Maddie fell into a peaceful slumber on the pile of clothing. He told himself that by now the sheriff and his deputies would have found not only Jerilyn and the other dead men, including Bo, and arrested Earl Ray Pitts.

It was over. Maddie was safe. Shane tried not to think about the future, especially about returning to the Texas Rangers. He felt healed emotionally and knew that had been Maddie's doing. He drew her closer, unable to face leaving her or Montana.

He'd barely finished the thought when a *whoop, whoop, whoop* filled the air. The cave went dark as a helicopter passed overhead, blocking out the sun.

Chapter Thirteen

"That's search-and-rescue looking for us," Maddie said, her eyes flashing open. She sat up abruptly and winced as she reached to rub her ankle. "We have to get up there."

Shane could see that her ankle was swollen and bruised, and as she reached for her clothes, she grimaced with pain.

"You're going to have to go without me," she said.

"I'll help you. I'm not leaving you here alone," he said, as he quickly dressed.

"No, the fastest way is to climb up the shaft," she said. "There is no way I can make it, but you won't have any trouble. There are footholds in the rocks. I think the Native Americans used this cave. You'll come out on top of the bluff. The view is incredible, and the chopper should be able to spot you up there."

He knelt down beside her. "Maddie…"

"I'll be fine." She gave him a quick kiss. "Go."

He pulled her to him and kissed her hard on the mouth. "I don't want you out of my sight until I know that Earl Ray Pitts is caught."

She smiled up at him, touching his cheek with her warm fingers. "You'll be right above me. If I need you, I'll yell. Once you flag down the helicopter, we can get out of here. I'm sure Earl Ray has already been arrested."

Shane hoped she was right. He told himself that Earl Ray was too big to get through the crack in the rocks and that he didn't even know about the cave. But Shane couldn't help but worry.

"Go and signal them. I'm starved," she said, giving him a playful push.

He laughed as he brushed his fingertips across her lips, knowing that if he kissed her again he wouldn't be able to go at all. "I'll be back with help as quick as I can. Don't try to climb out."

"Don't worry, I'm not going anywhere."

MADDIE WATCHED from below as Shane climbed up toward the sunlight. She smiled, remembering his kiss, his touch, their amazing lovemaking. The man could be as tender as he was powerful. Just the thought made her heart beat a little faster.

Hadn't she known that if she got close to Shane she'd fall for him like a rock off a cliff? She'd felt it the moment she saw him: that incredible chemistry, flashing like fireflies in the dark.

After Bo, she'd thought she'd never be ready to trust another man with her heart. Now she knew that it had just taken the right man. There'd been men at college who'd asked her out, but she'd felt no excitement, no rush of emotions. Just the sound of Shane's voice made her pulse buzz.

Maddie finished dressing, and not even her aching ankle could take away the euphoria she felt. Shane was almost to the top of the shaft and soon they would be back home. *But then what?*

Jud had told her that Shane was on a medical leave from the Texas Rangers, recuperating after being wounded.

"I'm hoping he decides not to go back to the Rangers," Jud had said. "Dad really wants him to stay here in Montana."

"As young as he is, he must have started training to get into the Rangers right out of high school."

"Yeah, he went straight into law enforcement while getting his degree. He always wanted to be a Ranger." There'd been a twinkle in Jud's eyes. "But if Shane found the right woman, a Montana cowgirl, I bet he'd think twice about going back to Texas. After he was shot, I think his priorities might have changed."

Talking about Shane and his love life had made her uncomfortable. Even then, she'd known she hadn't wanted to be the woman who kept Shane Corbett from his dreams. She could never let him give up the career he loved for her.

Shane reached the top of the shaft, called down to say he made it, and slipped over the rim and onto the bluff, disappearing from view.

Her heart lurched in her chest as she stared up after him, suddenly terribly afraid. She'd fallen in love with a man who would be returning to Texas to a job that could get him killed. *Had almost gotten him killed.*

She thought she heard the *whoop, whoop, whoop* of the chopper in the distance and another sound, this one much closer by—the sprinkle of tiny rocks.

Someone was coming up through the crack in the limestone—the same way she and Shane had climbed into the cave.

SHANE SPOTTED the helicopter over the Missouri River gorge. The chopper was flying low, no doubt searching for them. Or Earl Ray Pitts.

He moved to the edge of the bluff and waved his arms. Maddie was right. The view was breathtaking. He could see far down the river, limestone buttes towering on each side, the water slick with the sheen of the sun.

He thought about Maddie, twenty-five feet below him, and felt his heart soar at the memory of her in his arms. Was it possible that she was right about Jud setting them up? He didn't think his brother was that clever.

But if it was true, he owed his brother. Shane had never thought he'd ever meet anyone who could steal his heart, let alone his soul. He had fallen for Maddie so fast and yet fought it each step of the way. Until now.

He saw the chopper turn. The pilot must have seen him waving his arms, for the helicopter headed for him, the sound of the blades growing louder as it neared.

Shane couldn't wait to get back to Maddie. With help, they could get her out of the cave without further injuring her ankle. He just wanted to take her some place safe, feed her and let her get some rest.

He thought of Juanita's cooking. He'd take her to the ranch. He couldn't stand the idea of being away from her, especially not until he was sure Bo Evans was dead and Earl Ray Pitts was locked up for good.

Eventually he wanted to get her in a real bed, he thought with a grin. But he would always remember this cave and the way the light played on Maddie's face. He was still amazed at what he felt for her. No woman had ever gotten to him the way she had. Shane smiled to himself.

The *whoop, whoop, whoop* of the approaching helicopter got louder covering the sound of the man approaching from behind him.

MADDIE ROSE from where she'd been sitting to stand on her one good leg and lean against the rock face. Someone was definitely coming.

Through the shaft overhead, she could hear the chopper approaching. The pilot must have spotted Shane. But how did the person coming up through the crack in the rocks know she was here? There wouldn't have been time for search-and-rescue to see Shane and send someone up from below.

It had to be someone who knew about the cave, she thought, as she reached down and cupped a palm-sized rock in her hand.

Bo Evans slipped into the room and stopped when he saw her, looking around as if to assure himself that she was alone. She realized he must have been waiting until he heard Shane call down from the top of the bluff.

The look in Bo's eyes made her heart sink. She'd seen meanness there enough times. Last night she'd seen a sick kind of dangerous lust. But what she saw now was a cold, empty hatred that terrified her.

"You left me for dead," he said, his voice as dead as

his eyes. His clothes were caked with blood and dirt, and he moved oddly, holding his side with one hand. But he was still moving. Moving toward her.

Maddie said nothing. She knew there was nothing she could say to Bo. He'd always turned things around, skewing the truth to make him come out the victim. What had worried her was that he believed his own lies. They became more real to him than the truth.

"You made me fall for you and then you dumped me," he said, in that same inflectionless tone. "You deserve everything you get. I could have saved you. All you had to do was be just a little nice to me."

More lies. She knew now that it had been the vulnerability she saw in Bo that had made her stay with him as long as she had. That and the fact that, like her, he was flawed.

But she hadn't been able to save Bo.

All she could do now was try to save herself.

"What? No last words?" he asked.

She felt the rock in her hand and feared that she wouldn't be able to use it, as Bo moved in his odd shuffle toward her.

Maddie clutched the rock, knowing it had come down to either her or him. Bo had reached some new low that there would be no coming back from. That he'd brought his life to this point, he would never accept. He would blame everyone else. Call it bad luck. Finding peace only when he breathed his last breath.

His face twisted into something both evil and sad. "This is all your fault, Maddie. You only brought it on yourself."

He reached for her.

Maddie swung. The rock connected with Bo's head. He staggered back, looking confused, but still on his feet.

THE BLOW FROM BEHIND stunned Shane. He dropped to one knee on the smooth surface of the bluff as the chopper noise grew louder and louder, the sun glittering off the blades.

The kick to his kidneys dropped him all the way to the rock, but unlike the first blow, this one didn't come as a surprise. Shane quickly got back on his feet to face Earl Ray Pitts—the man he'd seen with Bo Evans the night of the rodeo dance—and the gun pointed at his heart.

"Just give me my property and I'll be gone," the big man said, motioning with the gun, an eye on the approaching chopper.

"What property would that be?"

"A small, black leather notebook." Earl Ray was studying him intently. "I know Jerilyn gave it to Maddie."

"I don't know what you're talking about, but I have a feeling you aren't going anywhere," Shane said. "I would imagine the sheriff is anxious to talk to you about Jerilyn's murder."

"It was an accident. The stupid broad fired the gun, trying to kill me, and ended up shooting herself. She shot and killed both of my men."

"I'm sure the sheriff will be glad to hear that." Shane could hear the helicopter. It was almost to him. He waited, knowing Earl Ray would look toward it.

When he did, Shane sprung, kicking the gun from Earl Ray's hand. The weapon skittered across the smooth rock. They both lunged for it, but before either of them could reach it, the pistol slipped over the edge of the shaft and dropped down into the cave.

Earl Ray leaped to his feet, charging like a mad bull, driving Shane to the brink of the cliff. Below was nothing but air for a good hundred feet, then a pile of huge boulders at the edge of the river.

The sound of the helicopter was deafening as it hovered just over their heads. Shane and Earl Ray teetered on the brink of the cliff, both struggling. Shane feared that Earl Ray wanted to take the coward's way out—the rocks below—rather than prison. Locked as they were in a death grip, it looked as if Earl Ray would take Shane with him.

He thought of Maddie and found renewed strength. Earl Ray was pushing him hard. He knew he stood only one chance against the man. Shane broke contact and, dropping to his knees, let Earl Ray's pressure tip him forward. Off balance, Shane levered the man over his back and over the cliff.

Shane felt Earl Ray grasping for something to hang on to. His fingers tried to clutch at Shane's sleeve, but Shane was already clambering away from the edge of the cliff.

Earl Ray dropped over the edge of the bluff. The chopper blades overhead drowned out the man's screams.

BO SHOOK HIS HEAD as if counteracting the effects of being struck by the rock. His right eye looked bloodshot, and the cut from where the rock had broken the skin on his cheekbone began to bleed.

But he stayed on his feet. For a moment he stood looking at Maddie as if he wasn't sure who she was. "You thought I didn't know about this cave." He let out a thin laugh. "I used to come here and get high when I was a kid. Then one day I saw you near here and knew you'd found my secret place. I hated you for taking it from me back then, and now I have even more reason to hate you."

Maddie gripped the rock in her hand until her fingers ached. He would come at her again, only this time he'd be expecting her to try to hit him again. He was stronger, larger, meaner than her. And the look in his eyes said he no longer had anything to lose.

A noise from above made them both look toward the shaft of light pouring into the room of the cave—and both started as the pistol hit the rock floor and bounced a couple of times before settling between them.

Maddie moved on pure instinct, hurling the rock at Bo as she lunged for the gun.

Bo let out a cry as the rock found its mark. She closed her hands around the grip of the pistol as Bo fell to the floor beside her. She rolled, her back to him, as she fought to keep the gun away from him.

He grabbed a handful of her hair, jerking her head back, and reached with his other hand for the gun.

She remembered the side he'd been holding when he came into the cave and drove her elbow back into him. Bo howled in pain. His one hand released her hair, his other drew back as if to clutch his wounded side.

Maddie rolled over, coming up with the gun gripped in both her hands. She was looking Bo Evans in the face. Her finger touched the cold steel of the trigger. She couldn't do it. Just like with the knife. She couldn't take another person's life.

"Can't do it, can you?" Bo bared his teeth, rearing back, fist clenched as he swung at her face.

Maddie fired twice, the shots echoing like thunder in the cave Then Bo Evans flopped face-first onto the rock floor of the cave.

From overhead, she heard Shane calling her name.

Chapter Fourteen

When Shane came into the room, Maddie looked up from the chair where she'd been waiting. She couldn't hide how nervous she was about the DNA results. She couldn't hide anything from Shane Corbett.

"Jerilyn Larch wasn't your mother," he said, stepping to her chair to pull her up into his arms.

Maddie hugged him tightly, fighting tears of relief. After a moment, she drew back. "But I don't understand. She knew so much about me."

"From what the sheriff has been able to find out, Jerilyn wasn't the only one to give birth that night at the hospital. Obviously, she got the wrong information."

Maddie blinked back tears as she looked into Shane's handsome face. Since that day in the cave, he'd been there for her every step of the way.

Sometimes at night she woke, imagining she heard the sound of the gun's report and could see Bo's face the instant before he died. Shane held her, soothing her with his words and touch. He was the one person who understood what she was feeling. He'd been fighting his own demons since killing the man who'd shot him in Texas.

"But Jerilyn was *someone's* mother," Maddie said. "She gave up her baby here in Whitehorse twenty-six years ago."

He nodded. "Honey, according to the sheriff, there were a group of older women who helped find homes for babies that the mothers couldn't keep. A secret adoption ring. The women took no money. They just wanted the babies to go to good homes. They truly believed they were helping both the mothers and the babies."

Maddie pulled away to walk to the window. Past the glass, the bright summer sun cast a golden glow over the land. In the green pasture, she could see her horse. Shane had brought it out to Trails West so she could ride once her ankle was better. The two of them had ridden every day since then, exploring the countryside, having picnics in the pines, talking for hours, or not talking at all. They'd become as close as any two people ever could.

"You're telling me that I was one of those babies," she said, not turning around.

"Your DNA also doesn't match Roy or Sarah Cavanaugh's."

She turned to look at him. "Then the other woman who gave birth that night was my mother?"

"That seems to be the case," Shane said quietly.

"So I have no idea who my mother or father was, where I came from, who I really am."

"We both know who you really are," he said, joining

her at the window. "A strong, intelligent, very sexy woman. What more do we need to know?"

She smiled, loving him more than words could ever express. "What if that's not good enough?"

"There might be a way to find out who your biological mother was and, from there, your biological father, if that's what you want to do. Do you still have the Whitehorse Sewing Circle baby quilt that you were given when you were born?"

Maddie frowned. "Yes, but why would…" Her eyes widened. "Are you telling me the older women who ran this adoption ring belonged to the Whitehorse Sewing Circle?"

"At least one member did. Probably more were involved. According to the sheriff, there is something in the stitches that tell who your birth mother was. The sheriff told me that the adoption ring is Whitehorse's long-time secret. No one knew about the clues in the quilt until recently."

Maddie couldn't believe this. She thought of how her mother had hated that quilt, had hidden it in the back of the closet, never using it. Now it made sense. In fact, so many things in her life were finally starting to make sense.

"I can't help but be relieved that Sarah wasn't my real mother, since she was such a terrible mother. Jerilyn certainly wasn't a step up. But I'm not sure I'm quite ready to find my biological mother," she said, smiling up at Shane.

"I'll support you no matter what you decide," he said, returning her smile. "There's something else. Buck

Jones found a small leather notebook hidden in a sugar canister at his house. He turned it over to the sheriff, who turned it over to the FBI. Apparently Earl Ray Pitts followed Jerilyn to Montana to retrieve this notebook. According to what the FBI has told the sheriff, the information in it could bring down a large segment of organized crime in Arizona and parts of Nevada."

"I heard Earl Ray ask Jerilyn about the book. That's why he killed her?"

"Earl Ray swore to me that it was an accident and that Jerilyn killed both of his men."

Maddie shivered and Shane drew her close, wrapping her in his arms. She snuggled against him.

"You did what you had to do," he said softly, as if he knew she was thinking of Bo.

She nodded. "It's just hard to think that I took his life."

"It's one of the reasons I'm not going back to the Texas Rangers."

She pulled back and looked at him in surprise.

He smiled. "You're the other reason."

"But you love being a Texas Ranger."

"*Loved.* I thought it was being shot that made me hesitant about returning. I'd worked so hard to get where I was, and yet I felt something was missing in my life." His gaze locked with hers. "I no longer feel that way. Nor do I feel driven to climb the ranks of the Texas Rangers."

"Are you sure about this, Shane?"

He nodded and smiled. "The sheriff has an opening for another deputy and said I have the job if I want it."

Shane took her shoulders in his big hands. "I told him it would depend on you."

"Me?"

"I love you, Maddie Cavanaugh."

"Could you say that again?" She'd waited to hear those words for so long.

He chuckled. "I don't take these words lightly. That's why I haven't said them until I could completely commit to you. I love you, Maddie Cavanaugh."

She smiled through her tears. "Oh Shane." To her surprise, Shane dropped to one knee. As he did, he opened his hand. In his palm rested a small velvet box.

Maddie blinked at her tears. "Shane?"

He opened the jewelry box. Inside was a beautiful diamond ring. "It belonged to my mother. As the first of the Corbett brothers to propose marriage, it is to go to my fiancée."

"Oh, Shane, I love it!" The ring was beautiful, and the fact that it had belonged to his mother made it all the more magnificent to her.

As he took her left hand, he said, "I haven't had time to have the ring sized, but—"

Both of them let out a gasp as the ring slid onto her finger—a perfect fit. Maddie met his eyes, hers overflowing. Shane looked as shaken as she felt. It was as if their love was meant to be. As if it were written in the stars. But neither of them believed in that, did they?

"Will you marry me?" he asked, his voice breaking.

She nodded and pulled him to his feet to wrap her arms around him. "Oh, yes, Shane Corbett. I so love you."

The room behind them filled with applause and

cheers as they both turned to find Shane's family gathered just inside the doorway.

"SOME THINGS are just destined to be, wouldn't you say?" Jud asked, grinning as he came into the room.

Shane saw that his other brothers were also grinning. Behind them his father looked close to tears. Kate was smiling, and everyone was looking as if they couldn't be happier—especially Jud.

"I have a bone to pick with you," Shane said to his brother. Jud had made himself scarce for weeks. He'd said he couldn't leave the film shoot in Canada, but Shane knew better.

"Just say thanks and let's leave it at that," Jud said, still grinning.

"Do you know what he did to me?" Shane asked the rest of his family.

"Are you kidding? He's been bragging about it ever since word spread that you'd asked Dad for the ring," Russell said.

"Yeah, let me guess who spread the word," Shane said, looking at his brother.

Jud laughed. "Took you long enough to figure it out. Hey, I'm a man of my word. I promised a wedding. I just didn't say it was going to be mine. The minute I saw Maddie, I knew she was perfect—for you. I knew it would be love at first sight."

Shane couldn't help but laugh.

"But I certainly hadn't planned on her being kidnapped," Jud added.

"I'm glad to hear that," Shane said.

"But you have to admit, you did come into her life right when she needed you—no matter what you say about destiny."

Shane scoffed. But he wasn't about to deny that he might never have met Maddie if things hadn't unfolded the way they had with his father remarrying and moving to Montana, and him getting wounded and ending up recuperating at Trails West.

"Well? Aren't you going to thank me?" Jud asked.

Shane shot him a warning look. "Don't push your luck. You still drew the shortest straw. You're the next one to get married."

"Hell, big brother, I have a whole year," Jud said. "A lot can happen in a year."

"This calls for champagne," Grayson said, as he and Kate came into the room to give Maddie a hug.

Shane watched as Kate hugged Maddie. He couldn't miss the tears in Kate's eyes as she pulled back to gaze into Maddie's face. "Welcome to the family, Maddie," she said, her voice breaking.

"About that champagne," Lantry said, going behind the bar to get one of the bottles that were chilling.

"I could use a stiff drink. I've had to listen to Jud brag for hours about his plan working," Dalton said, taking a stool at the bar.

Juanita came in with a tray of tiny tacos along with her homemade salsa, followed by Maddie's cousins and their husbands and Pearl and Titus Cavanaugh.

Shane watched his family, listening to the sound of laughter and the popping of several bottles of champagne. His gaze went to Maddie. Her face shone, those blue eyes brighter than he'd ever seen them. She'd been through so much, but she was strong. He had no doubt that she could take whatever life threw at her after this. Maybe even finding out who her birth mother really was, if that was what she decided to do.

Out of the corner of his eye, he saw his father move to Kate and put his arm around her. She was crying, her fingers pressed to her lips, her gaze on Maddie.

Shane felt a shiver move up his spine as he noticed how much the two women looked alike. They could almost be mother and daughter.

* * * * *

Mills & Boon® Intrigue
brings you a sneak preview of…

Debra Webb's
Secrets in Four Corners

*Sheriff Patrick Martinez is the law in Kenner County
and nobody is going to be threatened under his
watch – least of all his long-time love, Bree Hunter,
and her little son who he wished was his!*

Don't miss this thrilling first story in the
KENNER COUNTY CRIME UNIT
*mini-series, available next month
from Mills & Boon® Intrigue.*

Secrets in Four Corners
by
Debra Webb

Sabrina Hunter fastened her utility belt around her hips. "Eat up, Peter, or we're gonna be late."

Peter Hunter peered up at his mom, a spoonful of Cheerios halfway to his mouth. "We're always late."

This was definitely nothing to brag about. "But," his mother reminded him, "our New Year's resolution was to make it a point *not* to be late anymore." It was only January twelfth. Surely, they weren't going to break their resolution already.

Chewing his cereal thoughtfully, Peter tilted his dark head and studied her again. "Truth or dare?"

Bree took a deep breath, reached for patience. "Eat. There's no time for games." She tucked her cell phone into her belt. Mondays were always difficult. Especially when Bree had worked the weekend and her son had spent most of that time with his aunt Tabitha. She spoiled the boy outrageously, as did her teenage daughter, Layla. Even so, Bree was glad to have her family support system when duty called, as it had this weekend. She grabbed her mug and downed the last of the coffee that had grown cold during her rush to prepare for the day.

Peter swallowed, then insisted, "Truth. Is my real daddy a jerk just like Big Jack?"

Bree choked. Coughed. She plopped her mug on the counter and stared at her son. "Where did you hear something like that?"

"Cousin Layla said so." He nodded resolutely. "Aunt Tabitha told her to hush 'cause I might hear. Is it true? Is my real daddy a jerk?"

"You must've misunderstood, Peter." *Breathe.* Bree moistened her lips and mentally scrambled for a way to change the subject. "Grab your coat and let's get you to school." Memories tumbled one over the other in her head. Memories she had sworn she would never allow back into her thoughts. That was her other New Year's resolution. After eight years it was past time she'd put *him* out of her head and her heart once and for all.

What the hell was her niece thinking, bringing *him* up? Particularly with Peter anywhere in the vicinity. The kid loved playing hide and seek, loved sneaking up on his mother and aunt even more. His curious nature ensured he missed very little. Tabitha and Layla knew this!

Bree ordered herself to calm down.

"Nope. I didn't misunderstand." Peter pushed back his chair, carefully picked up his cereal bowl and headed for the sink. He rinsed the bowl and placed it just as carefully into the dishwasher. "I heard her."

Bree's pulse rate increased. "Layla was probably talking about…" Bree racked her brain for a name, someone they all knew—anyone besides *him*.

Before she could come up with a name or a logical explanation for her niece's slip, Peter turned to his mother once more, his big blue eyes—the ones so much like his father's and so unlike her brown ones—resolute. "Layla said my real daddy—"

"Okay, okay." Bree held up her hands. "I got that part." How on earth was she supposed to respond? "We can talk on the way to school." Maybe that would at least buy her some time. And if she were really lucky Peter would get distracted and forget all about the subject of his father.

Something Bree herself would very much like to do.

She would be having a serious talk with her sister and niece.

Thankfully her son didn't argue. He tugged on his coat and picked up his backpack. So far, so good. She might just get out of this one after all. Was that selfish of her? Was Peter the one being cheated by her decision to keep the past in the past? Including his father?

Bree pushed the questions aside and shouldered into the navy uniform jacket that sported the logo of the Towaoc Police Department. At the coat closet near her front door, she removed the lockbox from the top shelf, retrieved her service weapon and holstered it. After high school she'd gotten her associate's degree in criminal justice. She hadn't looked back since, spending a decade working in reservation law enforcement. The invitation to join the special homicide task force formed by the Bureau of Indian Affairs and the Ute Mountain Reservation tribal officials had been exactly the opportunity she had been looking for to further her career.

Besides her son and family, her career was primary in her life. Not merely because she was a single parent, either, although that was a compelling enough motive. She wanted to be a part of changing the reservation's unofficial reputation as the murder capital of Colorado. This was her home. Making a difference was important to her. She wanted to do her part for her people.

Not to mention work kept her busy. Kept her head on straight and out of that past she did not want to think about, much less talk about. An idle mind was like idle hands, it got one into trouble more often than not.

Enough trouble had come Bree's way the last few years.

No sooner had she slid behind the wheel of her SUV and closed the door had Peter demanded, "Truth, Mommy." He snapped his safety belt into place.

So much for any hopes of him letting the subject go. Bree glanced over her shoulder to the backseat where her son waited. She could take the easy way out and say his aunt and cousin were right. His curiosity would be satisfied and that would be the end of that—for now anyway. But that would be a lie. There were a lot of things she could say about the man who'd fathered her child, but that he was bad or the kind of jerk her ex, Jack, had turned out to be definitely wasn't one of them.

"Your father was never anything like Big Jack." Even as she said the words, her heart stumbled traitorously.

"So he was a good guy?"

Another question that required a cautiously worded response. "A really good guy."

"Like a superhero?"

Maybe that was a stretch. But her son was into comics lately. "I guess you could say that." Guilt pricked her again for allowing the conversation to remain in past tense…as if his father were deceased. Another selfish gesture on her part.

But life was so much easier that way.

"Am I named after him?"

Tension whipped through Bree. That was a place

she definitely didn't want to go. Her cell phone vibrated. Relief flared. Talk about being saved by the bell, or, in this case, the vibration. "Hold on, honey." Bree withdrew the phone from the case on her belt and opened it. "Hunter."

"Detective Hunter, this is Officer Danny Brewer."

Though she was acquainted with a fair number of local law enforcement members, particularly those on the reservation, the name didn't strike a chord. She couldn't readily associate the name with one department or the other, making it hard to anticipate whether his call was something or nothing. That didn't prevent a new kind of tension from sending her instincts to the next level. "What can I do for you, Officer Brewer?"

"Well, ma'am, we have a situation."

His tone told her far more than his words. *Something.*

When she would have asked for an explanation, he went on, "We have a one eighty-seven."

Adrenaline fired in Bree's veins. Before she could launch the barrage of homicide-related questions that instantly sprang to mind, Brewer tacked on, "My partner said I should call you. He would've called himself but he's been busy puking his guts out ever since we took a look at the…vic."

Damn. Another victim.

Bree blinked, focused on the details she knew so

far. Puking? Had to be Officer Steve Cyrus. She knew him well. Poor Cyrus lost his last meal at every scene involving a body.

One eighty-seven.

Damn.

Another murder.

"Location?" Bree glanced at her son. She would drop him off at school and head straight to the scene. Hell of a way to start a Monday morning. Frustration hit on the heels of the adrenaline. She'd worked a case of rape and attempted murder just this weekend. As hard as her team toiled to prevent as well as solve violent crimes it never seemed to be enough.

"The Tribal Park." Brewer cleared his throat. "In the canyon close to the Two-Story House. One of the guides who checks the trails a couple of times a week during the off-season found the victim."

"Don't let him out of your sight," Bree reminded. She would need to question the guide at length. Chances were he would be the closest thing to a witness, albeit after the fact, she would get. "Did you ID the victim?" She hoped this wasn't another rape as well. Twelve days into the New Year and they'd had two of those already. Both related to drug use.

Bree frowned at the muffled conversation taking place on the other end of the line. It sounded like Brewer was asking his partner what he should say in answer to her question. Weird.

"Ma'am," Brewer said, something different in his voice now, "Steve said just get here as fast as you can. He'll explain the details then."

When the call ended Bree stared at her phone then shook her head.

Damned weird.

"M-o-o-o-m," Peter said, drawing out the single syllable, "you didn't answer my question."

She definitely didn't have time for that now. More of that guilt heaped on her shoulders at just how relieved she was to have an excuse not to go there. "We'll have to talk about it later. That was another police officer who called. I have to get to work."

Peter groaned, but didn't argue with her. He knew that for his mom work meant something bad had happened to someone.

As Bree guided her vehicle into the school's drop-off lane, she considered her little boy. She wanted life on the reservation to continue to improve. For him. For the next generation, period. As hard as she worked, at times it never seemed to be enough.

"Have a good day, sweetie." She smoothed his hair and kissed the top of his head.

His cheeks instantly reddened. "Mom."

Bree smiled as he hopped out of the SUV and headed for Towaoc Elementary's front entrance. Her baby was growing up. Her smile faded. There would be more questions about his father.

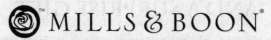

2 FREE BOOKS
AND A SURPRISE GIFT

We would like to take this opportunity to thank you for reading this Mills & Boon® book by offering you the chance to take TWO more specially selected books from the Intrigue series absolutely FREE! We're also making this offer to introduce you to the benefits of the Mills & Boon® Book Club™—

- **FREE home delivery**
- **FREE gifts and competitions**
- **FREE monthly Newsletter**
- **Exclusive Mills & Boon Book Club offers**
- **Books available before they're in the shops**

Accepting these FREE books and gift places you under no obligation to buy, you may cancel at any time, even after receiving your free books. Simply complete your details below and return the entire page to the address below. You don't even need a stamp!

YES Please send me 2 free Intrigue books and a surprise gift. I understand that unless you hear from me, I will receive 5 superb new stories every month, including two 2-in-1 books priced at £4.99 each and a single book priced at £3.19, postage and packing free. I am under no obligation to purchase any books and may cancel my subscription at any time. The free books and gift will be mine to keep in any case.

Ms/Mrs/Miss/Mr _____ Initials _____

_____

Surname _____

Address _____

_____

_____ Postcode _____

E-mail _____

Send this whole page to: Mills & Boon Book Club, Free Book Offer, FREEPOST NAT 10298, Richmond, TW9 1BR

Offer valid in UK only and is not available to current Mills & Boon Book Club subscribers to this series. Overseas and Eire please write for details.. We reserve the right to refuse an application and applicants must be aged 18 years or over. Only one application per household. Terms and prices subject to change without notice. Offer expires 30th June 2010. As a result of this application, you may receive offers from Harlequin Mills & Boon and other carefully selected companies. If you would prefer not to share in this opportunity please write to The Data Manager, PO Box 676, Richmond, TW9 1WU.

Mills & Boon® is a registered trademark owned by Harlequin Mills & Boon Limited.
The Mills & Boon® Book Club™ is being used as a trademark.